The Secret Summer of L.E.B.

The Secret

FOLLETT PUBLISHING COMPANY
Chicago

Barbara Brooks Wallace

Summer
of L.E.B.

illustrated by Joseph Cellini

ISBN 0-695-40481-4 Titan binding
ISBN 0-695-80481-2 Trade binding

Library of Congress Catalog Card Number: 73-93557

First Printing

To Mary and Sky and Sandy,
    For the love and the hours and hours
And to Lizabeth, my other sister

Chapter 1

THE THICK PLATE-GLASS DOOR lettered with the words *Winston Towers* opened with a soft sigh as Lizabeth, a small grocery sack in one hand, pushed against it with her shoulder. At seven-thirty in the morning, she was still the only other person in the lobby except for the desk clerk. Empty chrome and black leatherette chairs sat neatly around small chrome tables, ready for the day. Lizabeth hated the sight of them, but by keeping her eyes straight ahead, she could almost avoid seeing them. And by drawing a deep breath just before she came through the glass door, she could almost make it to the elevators without having to breathe in the stale smell of cigarette smoke.

Now, inside the elevator, Lizabeth pressed button number eleven. The door whished silently shut, and she rode up staring at the toes of her shoes. She never looked around in the elevator if she could help it. The mirrors on two sides always made her appear the color of the seasick-green padded-vinyl walls. She was happy that the ride was short and swift. In moments, the door had whished shut behind her, and she was running down the hushed, dimly lit hall to their apartment. The hall seemed to her a long, narrow, windowless cage. She always ran through it as if she were trying to escape from it.

"I see that the store was open," her mother said when Lizabeth dropped the grocery sack on the kitchen counter.

"Just!" Lizabeth said. "They had no blueberry yogurt, though, so I got the apricot. Will that be all right for your lunch?"

"Perfect, Sweetie. Apricot is fine." Her mother brushed a strand of long blond hair from her forehead and continued running the point of a small knife deftly around an orange. The knife had a dangerous Arabian Night's curve to it, Lizabeth thought, and looked as if it were carving up a small orange world. Her mother was an artist and did everything with neat, efficient hands. Lizabeth leaned on the counter to watch.

"Mother, I've decided," she said. "I want it to be red-and-white stripes like a candy cane. I believe that's what it *should* be, don't you?"

"What *what* should be?" her mother said absently. The knife moved steadily around the orange.

"The beach umbrella," Lizabeth replied, grinding her teeth slightly. She somehow felt her mother ought to know what she was talking about.

"Sweetie, would you please take Daddy a carton of skim milk for his coffee. I'll have these oranges sliced

8

in a minute." She paused. "Beach umbrella? What beach umbrella?"

Lizabeth sighed as she pulled open the refrigerator door. "For the summer house, Mother. You told me Grandmother and Great-grandmother always sat under one to keep their complexions fair. If we're going to stay in that very same house, things ought to be the very same way they were then. You said we'd have an umbrella and all the other things. Don't you remember? Mother, are you listening to me?" Lizabeth shut the refrigerator door and stood with the skim-milk carton clutched in her hand.

The small dagger had come to a stop halfway around the orange. Lizabeth's mother began staring down the garbage disposal as if she expected an eggshell or a potato peeling to speak to her. At the table, behind his morning newspaper, Lizabeth's father seemed suddenly to be hiding rather than reading. Lizabeth had experienced deadly silences like this one before, but for some reason, she was never ready for what came out of them.

"Mother?" she repeated.

Her mother set the knife down on the counter with great deliberation, as if she needed to find exactly the right location for it. "Lizabeth," she said, "we're not going to the summer house."

"Not going!"

"Sweetie, you don't have to be so—*loud*," her mother said. She wiped her hands nervously on a tiny pink finger towel she had safety-pinned to her cream-colored silk slacks.

9

"But what do you mean, *not going?*" Lizabeth asked desperately.

Before replying, her mother opened a cupboard and pulled out three floral bone-china eggcups, running a disapproving finger over the chipped edge of one cup. The eggcups were part of a set of Bracken family heirlooms. Lizabeth loved them wildly and didn't even feel they should be used, though her mother, she knew, didn't think much of them because they were old and the flowers on them faded. That was exactly why Lizabeth did love them.

"I mean we can't go, not this summer anyway," Mrs. Bracken said evenly.

"But, Mother, you and Daddy promised! You said we'd go the first summer we were here."

"We only said that we'd see."

"Well, *we'll see* means—it means—" Lizabeth stammered.

"Dear heart, *we'll see* means *we'll see.* It doesn't mean anything else."

To Lizabeth, the absence of the word *no* always meant the presence of the word *yes.* So *we'll see* had always meant something quite different to her than it did to her parents. Still, this did not seem like the time for a discussion of meanings.

"But why? You haven't told me why!"

"Daddy happens to have an important new job, that's why. He just can't get away."

Lizabeth whirled around. "Daddy, is that true?"

Her father lowered his newspaper to the table.

"True," he said. "Your mother is not having halluci-nations, Liza Belle."

Lizabeth knew that her father was only trying to be funny, but she didn't feel like even smiling about it. No one had the right to try to be funny over something like this. Furthermore, she had the terrible feeling that she was going to cry. In less than an hour, she was due to arrive at Anderson Bays School, and no-body in her right mind wanted to arrive at Anderson Bays School, or any other school, with eyes and face red and swollen from crying.

That was the trouble when bad news came so un-expectedly. Lizabeth had always felt that it should be preceded by black skies, lightning, and a horrible ap-parition in tattered garments howling at the windows, "Lizabeth Elvira Bracken, disaster is at hand! Prepare yourself!" That way, though you couldn't prevent the bad news, you could at least have your brain, and the pit of your stomach, ready for it.

As it was, her voice was already coming out drenched in tears. "Why—why didn't you tell me before?"

"Daddy simply wasn't certain until this week. Well, now he's certain. Anyway"—Mrs. Bracken gave a short laugh—"they'll be relieved at the gallery to find I'll be around all summer. Cheer up, Sweetie; we'll go another time. Perhaps next summer."

"But it's this summer that matters!" Lizabeth cried. "Daddy has his job. You have the art gallery. What about *me?*"

11

Mrs. Bracken's eyebrows arched. "For *you* there happens to be a very expensive swimming pool. In case you've forgotten, *it* is one of the reasons we took this apartment."

"You took it," Lizabeth hurled back, "because it was modern and convenient and—"

"And had a pool for you!" interrupted her mother firmly. "Come on now, Sweetie. You might have a perfectly delightful summer. Sharon will be home most of the summer, you told us, and you can invite her over to swim anytime you like. There are programs at the library and at the schools and playgrounds and—"

"Potholders!" Lizabeth burst out, her voice cracking dangerously again. "That's all they do at programs. I don't want to spend my whole summer making jersey p-p-p-potholders!"

Mrs. Bracken threw her hands up helplessly in the air. "Surely they must do other things."

"That's not the point," cried Lizabeth. "The point is not going to the summer house. I hate this apartment! I don't see how you can like it so much. It's just like living in a pile of plastic boxes at the grocery store. It makes me feel like—like an egg!"

Her father attempted a smile. "You don't look like an egg, Liza Belle."

Mrs. Bracken threw him a warning look, but it was too late.

"Oh! Oh!" Lizabeth choked. With a sob, she dropped the carton of skim milk on the dining table, and flung herself out of the room. The heavy, shining glass-topped tables, her mother's paintings on the walls,

12

the thick white-shag carpet under her feet, all blurred past her as she raced through the apartment to her room, slammed the door, and hurled herself down on her bed. She knew that she was behaving badly, like a spoiled brat, but she couldn't stop the scalding tears that spilled down her cheeks, making a large damp stain on her white quilted spread. She had wanted so much to go to the summer house that year. She was counting on it desperately.

From the time she could remember, Lizabeth had known about the Cartwright summer house. Her mother had been Julia Cartwright before she was married, and the house by the seashore in Massachusetts was where she had spent her summers as a young girl, and her mother before her, and her grandmother and great-grandmother.

The ornate Victorian house sat solidly and comfortably behind a covered veranda that spread out around it like a magnificent hooped skirt, making the house look like a complacent but very grand old lady, Mrs. Bracken said. It did look exactly like a grand old lady to Lizabeth in the snapshots, some almost faded away, that filled the family photo album.

And of course there were the wonderful words Mrs. Bracken used to describe the house, words like *gables* and *turrets* and even *gingerbread*. Before Lizabeth had learned that *gingerbread* meant the curled and twisted wood that decorated the eaves and veranda columns like stiff white Irish lace, she thought, naturally, it meant real gingerbread pulled from the oven and glued to the house. Lizabeth liked her own version better, so she halfway continued to believe it anyway, even now that she was older.

It wasn't only the description of the house that fascinated her. It was imagining all the things that had happened in it, and thinking of the large families that had come there, brothers and sisters and cousins and half-cousins. They must have had such glorious fun, Lizabeth thought. She imagined herself sitting on the veranda with them in the afternoon, sipping cool lemonades after a game of croquet. Perhaps, if she were with one of the later families, there would be records playing on a loud, scratchy Gramophone. At night, after supper, they would all walk down to the beach and go wading in the silver ripples, then return to the house, arms entwined, singing and laughing. Later, Lizabeth saw herself curled up in the window seat in her room, pajamas on and hair pinned up, reading until her mother came in to turn down—would it be a gas lamp? she wondered. Lizabeth rolled words over her tongue like *blackberrying* and *shelling* and *picnic hamper*. Food from a *picnic hamper* must have tasted far better than anything could from a *plastic cooler*. Even peanut-butter-and-jelly sandwiches.

Having her mother write and discover that the old house was now owned by people who might consider renting it to them for a month some summer made the move east more bearable for Lizabeth. Much more bearable! And now they were not going—not this summer, perhaps never. The words *perhaps next summer* seemed about as reliable to her as *we'll see*. They were lying words, all of them.

14

Tears finally stopped burning in her eyes, and she rolled over on her side, propped her face up with one hand, and stared dejectedly at the little desk across from her bed. She had wanted an old slant-top walnut desk that she had seen in a secondhand shop, but her mother had persuaded her it *wasn't* what she wanted, so they had bought this one to match the rest of her furniture. Like the other pieces, it had come from Denmark and been chosen by her mother for its smooth, simple lines and its clean, all-white finish. Except for two of Mrs. Bracken's paintings, airy daubs of cool blues and greens, on the wall over the bed, almost everything in the room was white.

It was definitely a room, Mrs. Bracken had said, that you could breathe in. Lizabeth had to agree, but still she did wish she had that old, battered slant-top desk with all the cubbyholes in it, and a little secret cupboard. What she liked best about her room now was her old dolls sitting across the bookshelf. And *those* she had to sweep off and hide in her closet each time she knew Sharon was coming to see her!

Lizabeth continued to lie on her bed, feeling her elbow grow numb where she leaned on it. She ought to be getting ready for school, she knew, but how could she go now with her eyes red and swollen? Hadn't her mother thought about that, throwing the bad news at her just when she had to go to school?

Her eyes drifted toward the closed door where her huge, floppy old cloth clown hung on a peg. Her mother had made him when Lizabeth was three, and he was really a laundry bag with a slit down the front

15

of his pink-and-red polka-dotted clown suit for putting in clothes. Lizabeth loved him, too, along with her dolls. Filled with laundry, he always looked fat and well-fed. But he had been emptied the day before, so now he hung limp and dejected from the door, his yellow cotton slippers with the silver bells on the toes drooping almost to the floor.

Then, as Lizabeth stared at the bells, she saw two slips of paper come sliding under the door beneath them. Slowly she rose from her bed, wiped her nose on her arm, and went to pick them up. They were both notes, as she suspected. She opened the first one and read:

For Mrs. Poole
Sixth Grade—Room 10
Anderson Bays School

Dear Mrs. Poole,

Please excuse Lizabeth's tardiness this morning. We had a family problem that needed to be settled.

Very truly yours,
Julia Bracken
(Mrs. Steven P.)

Lizabeth then unfolded the second note and read:

Dear Lizabeth,

When your eyes are dry and clear (cold water splashed over the face is very helpful for this,

16

Sweetie), and you feel that you are ready to go to school, you may take the accompanying note to your teacher.

I have telephoned the gallery to let them know I will be a little late this morning, so on your way out, please stop by the kitchen for:

a. A kiss.
b. Your lunch.

Julie Bracken
(*Your mother*)

P.S. Daddy wanted me to tell you that he is terribly sorry.

From the time Lizabeth was a very little girl, she had received notes like this second one from her mother, first with pictures, then later when she had learned to read, with words. It was a long time, though, since she had had one. She read it twice, and when she had finished, fresh tears poured down her cheeks. With both notes in her hand, she walked back to her bed, sat down, and stared once again at the silver bells on the toes of her laundry-bag clown. "Christmas bells for my baby," Lizabeth remembered her mother saying when she'd stitched them on, "so she'll always have Christmas in her room!"

Christmas forever and loving notes for the baby! But Lizabeth was only half-baby now. The other half was eleven years old, going-to-be-twelve-that-fall. Her mother and father could take care of the baby half, soothing the hurt feelings and the scraped knees. They would always take care of it. But the other half, the

17

growing-up half, had problems that neither Christmas bells nor notes could ever take care of. That half, Lizabeth knew finally, she would somehow have to manage all by herself.

She leaned over and laid the note addressed to her under her pillow. The one to Mrs. Poole she slipped inside her school notebook. Then she stood up and went to the bathroom to splash her eyes with cold water.

Chapter 2

LIZABETH RAN INTO CLASS at ten minutes after ten just
as everyone was beginning on their themes for an En-
glish test. The moment she handed her note to Mrs.
Poole and went to her desk, her friend Sharon began
sending silent messages across the aisle. Sharon formed
her mouth around the words "Send me a note!" and
widened her eyes so that rings of white framed her
pupils. She kept this up until Lizabeth finally skidded
a note across the floor in which she had for no logical
reason written, "Eye appointment." It was simply
something that had jumped into her head.

When the lunch bell rang, Sharon seemed hardly
able to wait until they were seated at the V.I.G.'s and
B.'s table to start pumping her for information. The
V.I.G.'s and B.'s were the Very Important Girls and
Boys in the sixth grade, most of them clustered to-
gether in Room Ten. Sharon was one of them, as well

as being a C.L., a Class Leader. Lizabeth sat at the table because she was a friend of Sharon's.

Lizabeth had never understood completely why Sharon had chosen her to be a friend when she had first come to Anderson Bays School in January. Before she and her mother and father had left California, Lizabeth had discussed with her best friend, Janey, the horrors of changing schools, especially in midterm. They had decided there were many things in the world that were wonderful when they were new—the satisfying smell of the inside of a new car, for example, the look of a new sweater before it got all messed up with wool pills and a stretched neck, the crisp feel of a new book when you opened it for the very first time, even a school textbook. But there was nothing good about being a new student, they decided. Neither one of them had ever had the experience, but they'd seen new students come into the school. Long ago, Lizabeth knew that she never wanted to be one.

For the first two days, it was as bad as she'd expected. She wanted to be invisible, but felt as invisible as a wart on the end of a nose as she listened to Mrs. Poole introducing her in the classroom. "Lizabeth and her family are living at the Winston Towers," Mrs. Poole informed her disinterested class. "Lizabeth was an honor student in her old school, students. She was secretary of her class this year. She was . . ." Etc. Etc. Clap, clap from the Room Ten sixth grade. Also snicker, snicker. Lizabeth's fingers felt like ice chips. Next to her sweater she felt sticky and wet. She was certain she wanted to die.

Then, on the third day, Sharon Eberhard widened

her big blue eyes in Lizabeth's direction and invited her home after school. One wave of Sharon's eyelashes, and Lizabeth had entered the magic circle of the V.I.G.'s and B.'s. Now she no longer scurried alone to the girls' room at recess like a scared rabbit. She went surrounded by a cluster of chattering girls. She didn't have to stand around alone on the school steps wondering what to do with her hands and feet until the bell rang. And most important, she sat at the V.I.G's and B.'s table for lunch every day. That was the biggest prize of all.

Today was the first time since the glorious day when Sharon had taken her arm at noon and said, "Come on, Lizabeth. You'll have to sit with us!" that Lizabeth wished she weren't there. What had happened that morning, then running all the way to school and coming into class late and breathless, made the day seem strange and unreal and as if it couldn't turn out right. It was like starting an old and familiar nursery game, then finding out you couldn't finish it properly because some of the bits and pieces were missing.

Dishes crashed in the school kitchen. Chairs scraped across the gray linoleum floor. Silverware clattered on aluminum trays, and the air filled with the laughter and squealing of Anderson Bays School at lunch. The noises swirling through the cafeteria had never seemed so loud to Lizabeth, nor the smells so thick. She felt as if she were having to swallow the smell like a warm, thick syrup along with her sandwich. It made her feel a little sick.

"You never told me you were going to be late," Sharon said. "Why didn't you tell me?"

"I didn't know, Sharon," Lizabeth said.

"You mean your mother didn't tell you you had an appointment?"

"She—I think she forgot."

"That's funny," Sharon persisted. "Mothers don't usually forget things like that."

Lizabeth took a nibble of her lettuce-and-cold-meatloaf sandwich, and wished there were some way to change the subject. Sharon was clearly going to go on and on about it, and one thing was certain—she didn't want to tell Sharon the real reason for her being late. Crying because she'd been told she wasn't going someplace for a summer holiday seemed even more babyish now that she was at school than it had at home. But more important, once when she had tried to tell Sharon how she felt about the summer house, and her daydreams about it, Sharon had laughed at her. One day soon, in a casual offhand manner, she might say, "Oh, by the way, we're not going away this summer," and that would be that. But she could not do it now.

"Are we going to trade today?" Lizabeth asked quickly.

Sharon's face went blank as it waited for her mind to catch up with the sudden change of subject.

"Trade? Trade what?"

"Oh, you know," Lizabeth said indifferently, "something from our lunches."

"Okay, sure," Sharon said. She leaned way over the lunch Lizabeth had spread on a piece of waxed paper in front of her. "What've you got?"

Before Lizabeth could answer, something that

22

looked like an apple core whizzed past between her ear and Sharon's forehead. Sharon and Lizabeth both looked in the direction from which they thought the missile had flown. Sharon's face was flushed and scowling as she searched the table for the guilty party. Almost everyone else at the table had by now determined that something interesting might be going to happen, and they were looking back and forth between Sharon and two boys who were guiltily digging around in their paper sacks at the end of the table.

The boys were Tom Leggett and Dennis Stickley. They were V.I.B.'s in the sixth grade, but Tom was also a C.L. Both boys were considered by Sharon, as well as other V.I.G.'s, to be *adorable*. Lizabeth wasn't quite certain what was adorable about either of them.

Dennis occupied a desk in class at the back of the room by the pencil sharpener. He greeted everyone who had the unfortunate need to sharpen a pencil with flat blue eyes, a twisted grin, and a big foot stuck out in the aisle. He would draw his foot back if you said, "Excuse me, please!" but Lizabeth always felt he was laughing at her when he did it. Dennis's two major talents were an ability to make loud belches and the ownership of arms and legs well trained to dart out like cobras and sock or trip anyone who wasn't on guard. Lizabeth never understood how he got away with so much except that he was terribly polite to grown-ups and called them all "sir" or "ma'am" to their faces. Mrs. Poole seemed to like this.

Tom Leggett wasn't nearly so bad, Lizabeth felt, at least when he was alone. The trouble was that he

23

hung around Dennis most of the time, which pretty much made them two of a kind.

Anyway, Lizabeth thought *adorable* was a funny word to apply to these two boys, or to any sixth-grade boys. It had always been a word she had thought of in reference to kittens or puppies. But she never said any of this to Sharon. As a friend of Sharon's, and therefore a member of the V.I.G.'s and B.'s, she knew she was expected to think as they did, or at least pretend to.

For a few moments, both boys kept their heads down and continued digging in their lunch sacks. Then suddenly, like two puppets on the same string, they both raised their eyes and grinned at Sharon. Dennis shrugged and jabbed a forefinger in the direction of someone sitting farther down the table from her. Echoing the smirk on Dennis's face, Tom nodded his approval.

Sharon whipped her head around in the direction Dennis was pointing. Lizabeth leaned forward so she could see who was supposed to have received the apple core. It was a boy sitting at the far left-hand corner of the table. His last name, according to the morning roll call, was Hunter. Mrs. Poole called him Douglas. The people Lizabeth knew called him C.D., which stood for Class Drip, or Creepy Douglas. They never called him these names to his face, though. Whenever they needed him, they usually just called him "Hey, you." He was the one person in the class Dennis wouldn't draw in his foot for at the pencil sharpener, no matter what was said.

The scowl on Sharon's face had actually already become a little put-on as soon as she realized who might have hurled the apple core. But when she had identified C.D. as the intended target, she turned and beamed a blinding smile in Tom's and Dennis's direction. Then she widened her eyes and formed her mouth around the word "Oh!" That put the seal of approval on it. The air of excited expectation that hung over the rest of the table died down instantly, and all went back to their tuna-fish sandwiches or chocolate-chip cookies or frankfurters and mashed potatoes and creamed peas on their cafeteria trays. Sharon went back to staring at Lizabeth's lunch.

Lizabeth took another quick look at C.D. and saw that even though his eyes were firmly fixed downwards on the paperback book he was reading, he was chewing his sandwich in a funny, awkward manner, and his face was flushed. She wondered what he was doing at that table anyway. There was nothing written into the school bylaws saying that the table by the corner windows was reserved for the V.I.G.'s and B.'s and their friends. But everyone knew it. Only someone else with a lot of nerve would sit at the table. Lizabeth wondered that Creepy Douglas didn't know better. Anyway, she was glad that something had happened to distract Sharon from questioning her about the morning.

"How about my banana for your apple?" Sharon said.

Sharon's banana was all speckled with brown spots and had a shriveled black stem. It looked as if it had been sitting on the Eberhards' kitchen counter for about two weeks. Especially today did Lizabeth not feel like eating that kind of banana. But she handed Sharon her apple without a blink, and when Sharon handed her the banana, she smiled a "thank you." Sharon smiled a "you're welcome" back at her.

"Would you like some of my sunflower seeds too?" Lizabeth asked.

Sharon pretended to study the apple in her hands. Then she turned suddenly to Lizabeth with a laughing look in her eyes. "I don't have three peanuts to exchange for them!"

It was about the tenth time Sharon had made this joke, and Lizabeth was getting tired of hearing it. She didn't think it was funny anymore. She hadn't even thought it was funny the first time, but she didn't want Sharon to know it. She made a sound that she hoped sounded like a laugh.

Lizabeth had told Sharon how she and Janey had worked out a system for trading things from lunches—half a banana for half an apple or orange, ten sunflower seeds for one peanut, nine raisins for one date, three thin carrot sticks for one stalk of celery. They even had special rules for cookie trades—anything with chocolate worth more, anything with walnuts worth less.

"I'll bet you did that in the fourth grade," Sharon had said when Lizabeth finished telling her about it. "That sounds like fourth-grade stuff."

Lizabeth never did tell her that she and Janey had been using the trade list up until the very last day she'd left school, in the middle of the sixth grade.

Sharon cracked a sunflower seed between her

teeth. "Now," she said, "I'm going to tell you what you missed this morning." Without waiting to hear if Lizabeth *wanted* to hear what she'd missed that morning, Sharon went on. "Well, the big thing is that our room has been chosen to represent the sixth grade in the Spring Festival variety show! Tom and I are in charge of getting the talent together. Mrs. Poole appointed us. I asked her if you could be my assistant, and she said it was fine with her."

"Thank you," Lizabeth said.

"Is that all? Don't you care that I asked?"

"Oh, yes!"

"You don't look like it."

"I do care, Sharon, honestly. That was very nice."

Sharon blew on what was formerly Lizabeth's apple, then rubbed it against her blouse sleeve. There was a funny blank look on her face. "Well, I could have asked somebody else."

"I know," Lizabeth said. She felt a sudden tightness in the middle of her stomach that had nothing to do with lunch or the cafeteria smells. "I am glad you asked me. I really am."

"Really?" Sharon turned to Lizabeth with a bright, warm smile. It surprised her, just as it always did when Sharon smiled at her that way. The tight feeling in her stomach vanished.

"Yes, really!" said Lizabeth.

Sharon began again eagerly. "Well, we're going to have lots of meetings. You know, things like that. I'll be letting you know about it after, well, after *Tom* and I have talked about it." She reached behind her neck and ran her fingers through her hair, giving what Lizabeth called the special girly-girly look.

Lizabeth tried to return it, and hoped hers looked real enough. She'd been practicing this look for some time now in front of her mirror, and thought she had it down pretty well. Once she'd been doing it unconsciously in the living room, rolling her eyes and smirking in the prescribed way, and her mother had noticed it and asked if she were feeling ill. Well, Lizabeth told herself, if she had to give loony looks like that to be a part of the V.I.G.'s and B.'s, she was going to do it.

Her look must have satisfied Sharon, because she barreled on talking about Tom and the pageant and Tom again, all in a secret, private whisper to Lizabeth. Only one thing happened briefly to interrupt all this. When Creepy Douglas got up to leave the table, someone next to Sharon said, "Good riddance to bad rubbish!" That seemed to be a hysterically funny thing to say among the V.I.G.'s and B.'s. Lizabeth herself thought it was pretty funny when it was directed at one of their own group, but for some reason didn't think it nearly so funny when used against someone else. But she laughed with everyone anyway and went right back to listening to Sharon.

Lizabeth had the strange feeling sometimes that everything she did now was exactly the opposite of how she felt. It was as if she wasn't even Lizabeth anymore. She wondered that she could still recognize herself in the mirror these days. Well, she thought, perhaps that was because she spent so much of her time practicing with the green eye shadow and lipstick she would be expected to wear to Sharon's B.B.P., her Big Birthday Party in June. All the V.I.G.'s were going to wear lots of makeup, Sharon said. So Lizabeth knew that she would too.

Was life from now on going to be one long session of being something she wasn't, saying things she didn't mean, and acting ways she didn't always like? Lizabeth wondered. She had had the experience of feeling left out and unwanted. She had been on the *outside* for a few days, and never wanted to be there again. Now she had entered the magic circle of the V.I.G.'s and B.'s. She was on the *inside,* and she liked it. It frightened her to think sometimes how easily she could be outside again.

So "Yes!" in answer to all those questions. She would say what she needed to, and act the way she was expected to, to stay where she was, even if it meant being someone besides Lizabeth Elvira Bracken.

Or was it now L.E.B.? Perhaps she ought to be initials too, along with everything else.

Chapter 3

BY THE END of the school day, Lizabeth felt much better. The sick lump she'd developed in the cafeteria was gone. She had managed to forget about the summer house for a while, and Sharon seemed to have forgotten about her being late to school that morning. But as they were walking down the hall together that afternoon, arms wrapped around their books, Sharon said, "I was going to invite you over to my house today, Lizabeth, but I'm going to be busy."

"Oh," said Lizabeth, for lack of anything better to say.

"Don't you want to know what I'm going to be busy doing?" Sharon asked sharply.

"I didn't know you wanted to tell me," Lizabeth replied.

"You didn't even ask!" Sharon shot back.

"I didn't—" Lizabeth hesitated. "Please tell me, Sharon! I really would like to know."

Sharon blew a stray curl away from her mouth, and stared stonily ahead. "Well, I don't know why I ought to tell you things when you keep things from me. You ought to tell your *best* friend everything, Lizabeth."

A hint of her earlier sick feeling crept back into Lizabeth's stomach. They seemed to be right back where they'd started. "What didn't I tell you, Sharon?" Lizabeth asked.

Sharon threw her a sideways look. "About this morning."

"But I told you, I had an eye appointment."

"Yes, but you changed the subject at lunch. *I* wasn't fooled," Sharon said with a knowing look. "Anyway, you've been acting—funny all afternoon. People don't act that way just from having an eye appointment, unless they've heard something terrible." Sharon's eyes widened suddenly. "Did the doctor tell you you had to have glasses?"

"Yes," said Lizabeth.

Sharon looked stricken. "That's too bad. Well," she continued blithely, "since you've told me what really happened this morning, I guess I can tell you that Mrs. Spitz is giving makeup lessons in baton twirling. If I get done in time, I'll call you. Okay?"

"Okay," said Lizabeth, hoping she sounded pleased enough to satisfy Sharon.

"Remember about best friends not having secrets," said Sharon, widening her eyes as if to let Lizabeth know how important that was. "I'll try to call you later."

She smiled at Lizabeth. Lizabeth smiled back, and

they waved good-bye at the school door as if nothing at all had happened.

But the day had become hateful again to Lizabeth. Her brain ached with wondering why friendship with Sharon suddenly seemed so difficult.

Best friends! Sharon had said that twice in a row. Why did it make her feel so miserable?

In the soft, melting spring weather, it seemed as if the whole school were staying to play on the school grounds. Clouds of May dust flew up around the baseball diamond as the blue-jeaned bottoms of fourth- and fifth-grade boys scraped the ground on the way to first base. Hopscotch had just been rediscovered at Anderson Bays, and seven furious games were in progress on the blacktop. Every swing was in motion; every piece of play equipment was in use. "I see London, I see France, I see somebody's underpants!" chorused four grinning little boys. Too engrossed in flying higher or in getting to the other side, the little girls paid no attention to them.

Lizabeth watched enviously as three girls made their way across the swinging bars. At Anderson Bays, it seemed that you didn't do things like that once you were past the fifth grade, especially if you were a V.I.G. Back home, she and Janey had always swung on the bars. They had done lots of things together, but most important, they had shared their thoughts and their secrets. Janey was a real best friend. The words meant what they were supposed to with her. When Sharon said *best friends,* it sounded more like a threat.

Lizabeth hurried from the playground because she

32

couldn't bear to stay there any longer. But once she had left the paved path that bordered the school, her footsteps slowed. Though there was no place else for her to go just then, she knew she didn't want to go home. Going home meant walking through the Winston Towers lobby, being enclosed in the Winston Towers elevator, and finally sitting trapped in her Winston Towers bedroom. She decided that today she would take the long way home, and make it last as long as possible.

The long way carried her into a world different from the one around the Winston Towers, with its grocery stores, gasoline stations, and all-night drugstores. Lizabeth dawdled aimlessly along the tree-lined streets, wondering that the air should smell so sweet here, or that birds should be spinning a web of song over her head. It seemed almost like being in the country.

Her feet slowed and then finally stopped before a very large lot almost the size of a small park. A deserted old frame house, a curious contrast to the other sturdy brick houses on the street, stood near the back of the lot, its vacant, staring windows crisscrossed with boards. The house hardly showed at all, even in deep winter when the trees and shrubs around it were bare. Now rapidly growing leaves made it seem that the house would soon disappear altogether behind a curtain of green.

The idea that this wild, uncared-for piece of land should be allowed to develop as it pleased had been strangely exciting to Lizabeth. Most of the gardens she had known were so organized. At Winston Towers, the plants in the lobby were green plastic. But she had never thought too much about the half-hidden old house behind the trees. Today, because old houses were very much on her mind, she did think about it, wondering who might have lived there and if someone would ever live there again. Suddenly, she decided that she must see it from up close, to stand in front of it and look up at it.

There was no sign anywhere to tell her she shouldn't see the house if she wanted to. The quiet street was empty, so there was no one to be curious about what she was doing or to ask questions. Still, she had never done anything quite like this in her whole life, even with Janey, and her heart drummed out short, sharp beats in her chest as she clutched her books tightly and started down the brick path to the house.

The path had long since fallen into disuse. Lizabeth had to step around places where bricks were crumbling or missing, threading her way carefully through ivy and honeysuckle that crept across the path in tangled, twisted ropes. Then the path began to curve, and in only a few moments, she felt completely hidden from the street. Trees—tall, slender oaks and black walnuts—met like a cathedral arch over her head. Sunlight broke through only in tiny spots, dappling the path so that it looked as if a brush of yellow paint had been spattered over it. The air had the faintly damp smell of wet bricks and plants growing luxuriantly, as if they were in a hothouse—the *green* smell, Lizabeth had always called it. She took in deep breaths as she made her way through it.

The path curved again, and after only a few steps more, Lizabeth was standing before the old frame house, which seemed to have sprung through the moss and dead leaves around it like a shabby gray mushroom. It was much smaller than she had imagined it, for all of its two stories. But she was only looking at the back of the house, Lizabeth decided. A tipsy screen door, half off its hinges, looked as if it led into a kitchen. She continued on down the path, staring up at the house, and discovered that she was right. The front of the house was at the back, with a veranda stretching from one end to the other. From the veranda, the land sloped rather steeply downward, disappearing quickly in a thick forest of trees and wild shrubs.

Strangely, the windows on that side of the house had no crossed boards over them, so it didn't look nearly so desolate. Still, the veranda sagged. Most of the once-white paint had long since peeled away, and all the shutters hung at crazy angles from the windows. It was the sad shell of a house, and yet Lizabeth felt curiously peaceful standing in front of it, with the tall trees shutting out the world around them. It was like being in a glade in the middle of a forest. She even thought she could hear water running someplace, a brook or a spring.

Then suddenly, sharp, snapping sounds like the bursting of small firecrackers shattered the silence. Lizabeth stiffened with fright, but almost with her next breath, sighed with relief and smiled. "Oh, it's only you," she said, addressing a squirrel bounding across the dry twigs in front of the house.

The squirrel scurried up and perched on the lowest limb of an oak tree, stared at Lizabeth for a moment, then twitched his tail and bounded back down again. Crossing the path, he darted up onto the veranda railing and sat there, examining Lizabeth with wily black eyes.

Lizabeth couldn't help laughing aloud. The squirrel seemed so much at home on the veranda, as if he actually lived there and were inviting her up to see it. Another flick of the tail, and he ran around the railing and took a flying leap onto a window ledge. He turned again toward Lizabeth and tilted his head questioningly. The invitation was so clear, it seemed almost rude not to accept it.

"All right," Lizabeth said, laughing again, "I'll come!"

The steps to the veranda were thickly carpeted with leaves. They felt soft and slippery under Lizabeth's feet. She put one foot carefully ahead of the other, holding tightly to the railing with one hand. The veranda tilted much more than she had imagined. At the top, Lizabeth felt as if she were on a rolling ship. But though the wood creaked, it felt sturdy enough, and she walked carefully to a window on the opposite side of the door from where the squirrel sat. She laid her school books on the floor, then stood up, curled her fingers around the window rail just at the top of her head, and pressed her nose against the glass.

The room she saw beyond the window stretched from one side of the house to the other. It must have been the living room, Lizabeth thought. Still *was* the living room, except that no one was living there. Sunlight poured through the crossed bars of windows on either side of a brick fireplace to her left, making bright pools of light on the floor. Two chairs, one a straight-back kitchen rocker and one a lumpy wicker rocker, both with no cushions, sat in the middle of the room, looking as if they were having a conversation with one another. Stringy lace curtains hung like stiff pokers at the sides of all the windows. Beyond these things, the room was bare of furnishings. Rumpled newspapers and old rags littering the floor made the room look not so much empty, as deserted.

Still, anything at all in the room gave Lizabeth a funny feeling. Somebody had sat in those chairs once. Somebody had hung the curtains and even strewn the papers and rags on the floor. Now they were gone. Forever? she wondered.

She was never quite certain afterwards how it happened, except that she must have been pushing up on the window rail without knowing it. But suddenly the window squeaked and shifted upwards an inch. With a small sound of fright, Lizabeth jumped backwards. Then, when she realized that *she* was the one who had lifted the window, she stared at the gaping inch of space, and stepped towards it again. Almost as if she were in a trance, she put her fingers under the window. It squeaked, groaned, and slid all the way up. She slipped one leg over the window ledge. The splintered wood scraped her skin where her knee sock ended, but she didn't stop. She lifted her other leg, slid over the ledge, and dropped to the floor.

The odd thing, she remembered later, was that none of what she was doing seemed dangerous, or frightening or even wrong. She had the feeling that she *might* be a garden-trespasser, and she was most certainly a housebreaker. Yet none of it seemed to matter. All that mattered was that she was in the house. She sank to the floor by the fireplace, drew up her knees to her chin, and gazed around the room.

How very quiet it was inside the house, she thought. *Silent* was a better word. There was no rushing of air through a heater vent, no buzzing of a refrigerator. It was absolute stillness. And peace. It was as if time had stopped, and she could stop right along with it.

The room, of course, was terribly dirty, much more so than Lizabeth had been able to see through a window filmed with dust. But a good sweeping would help immensely, she thought. So would scrubbing down the walls and washing the windows.

The room had a pungent, sour smell about it, however, even though it was pleasantly warm and dry from the sun. Lizabeth wondered where she had ever smelled anything like it before, and then remembered. When her Great-Aunt Edith had died, they'd been sent a whole trunk of old, interesting things that her mother and father told her were family heirlooms. That was when they had got the bone-china eggcups. In the trunk was a package of two one-hundred-year-old family Bibles, as well as a tattered velvet box containing six blue enamel teaspoons. The Bibles, the velvet box, even the insides of the trunk itself, had all had this same smell. "Old age," Mrs. Bracken had said. "Mildewy old age."

That's what this house smelled of—old age, Lizabeth decided. Open windows would take care of most of it. But not all of it, she added quickly to herself. Some of it should certainly remain there. She rather liked it.

She hugged her knees tightly against herself, staring at the floor. Then she began dreamily to draw half-moons in the dust. She drew three of them. They looked like smiling mouths, so she put circles around them. Then she added dots for eyes, and larger dots for noses. She ended up putting on necks and bodies and arms and legs. Lizabeth was not much of an artist, to the despair of her mother, and these were the same stick figures she had been drawing since practically before kindergarten. She started to wipe them away, and then remembered that no one would be seeing them but herself. They would be there to welcome her the next time she came to the house.

The next time she came to the house, Lizabeth repeated to herself in the same dreamy way she'd drawn the stick figures. But then, there was really nothing so surprising about it. She seemed to have known all along that she was coming back, from the time she had started down the vine-covered brick path. Suddenly the whole day began to make sense to her, as if she had found the missing pieces to the nursery game. It was the "if" game. If she hadn't been told they were not going to the summer house, she would never have cried. If she hadn't cried, she would not have been late to school. If she hadn't been late to school, things might not have gone so badly with Sharon, and she would not have dawdled along playing guessing games with houses. She would never have come into the wild garden or accepted the squirrel's invitation into the house. The pattern of the whole day had fallen into place.

Now it was—Lizabeth looked at her little gold watch—four-thirty! She had left school over an hour ago, and she had promised she'd call her mother at the gallery when she got home. More than that, what if Sharon called *her?* What story would she have to make up to tell Sharon? She already knew that she wasn't going to tell Sharon about the house. If Sharon hadn't understood about the summer house, how would she understand about this one? The house ought to be shared with someone, but there was no one to share it with, no one except the squirrel.

Lizabeth jumped up and dusted off her skirt. Then she hesitated, looking through open glass doors that led into another room as bright and sunny as the one she was in. She wondered if she should take a few moments to explore the rest of the house. But she decided that she wouldn't. Strangely, though she hadn't been frightened until then, the idea of going past the front room did frighten her. A room in the back, the kitchen she thought it was, looked so much darker than where she stood. She would explore another time, she told herself, when she was more used to the idea of the house. After all, she had a whole summer ahead of her for that! With one last look around the room, she climbed out the window and carefully closed it behind her.

She hoped that the squirrel would still be sitting on the window ledge so that she could wave to him. But the ledge was empty, and the squirrel was gone. She would have to tell him when she came back that the house belonged to both of them now.

Chapter 4

LIZABETH had trouble falling asleep that night. All the things that hadn't seemed to worry her when she went to the house began to worry her then. As she lay staring at the tiny sparks of light winking at her from the silver bells on the toes of her clown, all the adult logic that her mother and father might apply if they knew about the house spun through her mind. "Sign or no sign, you should not have gone into the house. It was trespassing!" "Prowling around an old, vacant house alone. Supposing you fell and hurt yourself!" "And what if there were someone hiding there, someone dangerous? What then, Lizabeth Elvira Bracken?"

And Lizabeth knew that they would be right. The house must surely belong to *someone*, so it was wrong to go there, wasn't it? And in her bed, alone in the dark, she felt a cold chill in the middle of her stomach at the thought of having been alone in the house. Or had she even been alone? Couldn't someone have been lurking in a dark corner someplace? She had probably been very smart not to go exploring. Now she never would, because she was, of course, never going back there again. That was the last thing she remembered thinking when she finally closed her eyes to shut out the lights from the silver bells, and drifted off to sleep.

But in the morning, when she threw open the blinds to her room and the sunlight flooded in, none of the warnings she had given herself the night before seemed important at all. Before her mother and father were up, she had gathered together paper towels and rags, had filled a small plastic bottle from her travel kit with window cleaner, and had put all these things into a paper sack. When she left for school that morning, she carried the sack hidden under her school books. She was going back to the old house just as she had known she would when she sat drawing stick figures in the dust.

As she made her way down the worn brick path, Lizabeth decided that she was perfectly right in coming back. And it was all so beautifully familiar this second time. The spindly oak tree with the short, stubby limbs was waiting for her. So was the thick clump of ferns and the three pine seedlings that looked like tiny Christmas trees. She looked for and found the bright green patch of furry moss covering the north side of an old tree stump. She even remembered the place in the path where two bricks were missing, where she had nearly fallen the day before.

As she rounded the curve in the path, she dropped suddenly to her knees and scooped up a handful of acorn cups that lay over the carpet of dead leaves. She thrust them into the paper sack, and then gathered nine small pinecones and a pink granite rock the size and almost the shape of a turkey egg. Then, before continuing down the path, she twisted off two small branches from a scrubby white pine tree, putting them on top of her school books because they were too big to stuff into the sack. The wonderful fresh pine smell made up for the way they scratched her arms.

The squirrel was sitting on the lowest step of the veranda as Lizabeth rounded the corner of the house. When he saw her, he bounded up the steps and leaped to the railing.

"Good morning," Lizabeth sang out to him. "Good morning—Squirrel Nutkin!"

The squirrel flicked his tail twice and tilted his head questioningly.

Lizabeth laughed. "Well, you *should* have a name, and that's the name of another squirrel, a quite famous one if you care to know. He's the hero of a book. Anyway, I've come to leave some things at our house before school. I hope you don't mind." The squirrel gazed steadily at her with bright eyes. He gave the definite appearance of understanding what she said.

The leaves under Lizabeth's feet crunched softly as she went up the veranda steps. Without hesitating, she went to the window she had climbed through the day before, and lifted the sash. She dropped the paper sack and the pine branches over the sill into the room, and after laying her school books on the veranda floor, climbed into the room herself.

The rocking chairs still sat peacefully in the middle of the floor. The stick figures lay in the dust untouched, smiling vacantly at the ceiling above them. The early-morning sun poured through the front windows, drenching the room with light. Lizabeth wondered how she could ever have thought she was afraid to come back, except that she had thought it alone at night in a dark room.

But this morning she had no time to daydream or begin cleaning the room, because she had promised Sharon that she'd be to school early. She had time for only one thing. Picking up the paper sack and the pine branches from the floor, she carried them to the fireplace. Then she pulled a rag from the sack, and with one great sweep across the top of the mantel, wiped off the thick layer of dust. Suddenly, there were thousands of dust particles dancing and swirling in the sunlight. Lizabeth took a moment to fill her cheeks with air and blow into them, fascinated by the tiny tornado of dust she could make.

With the dust still whirling around her, she dipped her hand into the paper sack again, and quickly, one by one, lifted out the acorn cups, the pinecones, and the egg-shaped pink rock. She arranged the pinecones carefully on the left side of the mantel. The pine branches she laid to the right, opposite the cones. In the center of the mantel she placed the rock, circling it with a ring of acorn cups.

46

Satisfied with her work, she picked up the paper sack with the rags, paper towels, and bottle still in it, folded down the top, and set it in a corner by the fireplace. Then she ran to the window. With one leg over the sill, she turned once more to look toward the mantel.

They looked beautiful, she thought, her first gifts to the house. The rock, the ring of acorn cups, the pine branches and cones, all seemed magical on the mantel, as if someone had cast a spell on the house. It was she, Lizabeth Elvira Bracken, who had done it, making the house hers.

"You're late!" Sharon said to Lizabeth. She was standing with Betsy Farrell, Martha Cambridge, and Dody Green on the side of the school steps reserved for V.I.G.'s and B.'s. "You said you'd try to be early."

"I did try," Lizabeth said breathlessly. "I ran all the way."

"Oh," said Sharon. "Well, listen to what Betsy and Martha and Dody and you and I are going to do for the variety show. We're going to—"

Betsy and Dody interrupted her with a howl. "Let Martha tell Lizabeth, Sharon. It's *her* idea!"

"Okay," Sharon said willingly. "But wait until you hear it, Lizabeth. It's the cutest thing!"

"Oh, it's not that good," said Martha, flushing with pleasure.

"Yes, it is!" Dody broke in quickly. "It's darling! Go on, tell Lizabeth."

"Well," began Martha, "we'll all come on the stage doing the Charleston—"

Dody started wiggling her feet on the steps. "That's this dance where—"

"Shut up, Dody," Betsy interrupted, "and let Martha finish."

"And we'll all end up singing 'By the Beautiful Sea,' " said Martha, rushing through her recital.

Dody began dancing again and singing, "Da da dum, da da dum, da da da da da dum!"

The girls all groaned, laughing at the same time.

"Dody, come on!" Betsy said. "We don't want anyone to find out about it just yet and copy us. Anyway, what do you think, Lizabeth? Isn't it going to be fun?"

Lizabeth nodded, smiling. She did think it was, and she was happy to be included in it. "Will we have costumes?" she asked.

"Costumes!" Dody shrieked and grabbed her head. "Costumes! Tell her, somebody."

"We're going to be dressed as flappers," Sharon said. "You know, dresses with long waists and short skirts, and bands around our foreheads."

"And beads, beads, beads," sang out Dody, "all the way down to our belly buttons!"

"If we can get them," Martha said.

"Belly buttons?" asked Dody.

"Beads, stupid," said Martha, giggling.

"They're expensive, even plastic ones," Sharon said. "I mean, if we have to have a lot of them."

"At Christmas—" Lizabeth began excitedly, and then stopped.

"At Christmas what, Lizabeth? Come on, tell us," Sharon said.

Lizabeth hesitated. "It might look silly. But at Christmas I always string popcorn for our tree. Sometimes I color it with Easter-egg dye. I thought that—that maybe we could make popcorn beads. Oh well, I guess it's a dumb idea." She stopped in confusion.

"Dumb!" Dody exploded. "I think it's an adorable idea!"

"I do too, Lizabeth," Martha said. "Popcorn hardly costs anything, and we'll have fun making the beads."

"They won't jingle like real beads," Lizabeth said shyly.

"Who cares!" Betsy told her. "We'll make enough noise anyway."

Dody began jumping up and down. "The Pop-Pop Girls, that's what we'll call ourselves, the Pop-Pop Girls by the Sea. Next to Martha's idea about doing the Charleston and being flappers, Lizabeth's idea about popcorn beads is the most geniusy one of the day!"

Sharon smiled and patted Lizabeth on the head. "That's my friend, Lizabeth Bracken, the genius!"

"What about our dresses? Does anyone have any geniusy ideas about them?" Betsy asked. "I mean, are we actually going to have to *make* them? Stringing popcorn is fun, but sewing dresses? Ugh!"

"I sew a little," Martha said. "Anyway, our mothers will probably help us. They usually do if we look sad and helpless enough."

"Don't worry—we will!" Dody said. "But where are we going to get the stuff to make them with? Doesn't material cost a lot of money?"

"Everybody's mother has some old formals or party dresses hanging around," Sharon said. "We ought to be able to find something we can cut down to fit us."

Betsy grinned. "Another genius in our midst!"

"Hey, look," Dody announced suddenly. "Here come the boys! Let's tell them what we're going to do. *They* can't copy it!"

Five V.I.B.'s, including Tom Leggett and Dennis Stickley, were crossing the blacktop toward them.

"Hey, guess what?" Tom said before any of the girls had a chance to speak. "*We're* going to have a washboard band for the variety show." He looked around smugly.

The girls exchanged blank glances. Betsy wrinkled her nose. "What's that?" she asked.

"It's neat," Bob Weiss replied. "We'll play stuff like tissue paper over combs, and a tin tub for a drum, rubbing a stick over a washboard, all that kind of jazz. We thought maybe you girls would like to do it with us."

"Ugh!" said Dody. "Anyway, we already know what we're going to do. Tell them, Martha."

Martha didn't need a second invitation this time to explain her idea.

"Sounds pretty good," Tom said. "Singing, and all that."

"Well, we were going to sing too, weren't we, guys?" Hank McGinnis said defensively.

The boys didn't look as if they had even thought about it, but they gave each other wise looks and said, "Sure, sure we were."

The girls laughed approvingly.

50

"Tom," Sharon said, "why don't you play your trumpet, too?"

Dennis immediately began taking little mincing steps around Tom. "Come on. Play your trumpet, Tom!"

"Oh, shut up, Dennis," Dody said. "We girls think you should, Tom. It might improve your uggy washboard band."

Tom grinned. "If you think so, maybe I will."

"What about the rest of the class? What are they going to do? Do you and Sharon know yet?" Hank asked Tom.

"Mrs. Poole said we could take a class period today to talk about it," Tom told him.

Sharon raised her eyebrows at the group. "She says she wants everyone in the class to par-ti-ci-pate."

"Even people like C.D.?" squealed Betsy. "What can he do?"

"Clean-up crew," Dennis said.

Betsy threw him an arch glance. "You'll need someone to clean up after you!"

"Yuk! Yuk! Yuk!" replied Dennis.

"No, I mean it," Betsy said. "What's he going to do?"

"What else? Stink up the show," said Dennis, punctuating his reply with a loud, juicy belch.

"Oh, honestly, Dennis!" Betsy said, but she laughed along with everyone else.

The bell rang, and Dody skipped up the steps ahead of the rest, dancing and singing, "Do do de-o, Dody!"

"Hey! Hey!" Tom called after her.

Laughing, they all ran up the steps behind Dody.

Lizabeth found herself laughing too. Despite some of the things she'd been thinking the day before, it was fun belonging to this group. She couldn't help thinking again how lucky she was.

Actually, the whole day was fun. After school, Martha invited the four other girls over to her home to pop and string corn for their costumes, though, as Dody said, they ended up eating a lot more than they strung. The popcorn party kept Lizabeth from returning to the house to begin her cleaning as she had planned to do, but she didn't mind. A whole free Saturday lay before her, and she would go then.

When the popcorn party ended, Sharon invited her home for dinner. They spent the evening digging out some of Mrs. Eberhard's old high-school formals from a trunk and trying them on, giggling hysterically at the way they hung on Lizabeth's skinny frame. On the way to the Winston Towers in the Eberhard car later that night, Sharon squeezed Lizabeth's arm and said, "Didn't you think today was great, Lizabeth?"

"Oh, yes!" said Lizabeth, and she was certain Sharon knew that she meant it.

She had come very close several times to telling Sharon her secret, but she hadn't in the end. Yes, they'd had a very good time together, but it was still Sharon's kind of fun they'd been having, just as it always was. She wasn't going to risk letting Sharon laugh at her again, or make fun of her discovery. The old house in the trees would have to remain her very own, very safe secret.

52

Chapter 5

SHE WAS THERE, she was really there, and it was the beginning, Lizabeth told herself.

She was sitting on the middle step of the stairs going up to the veranda of the house, her chin resting on her bare knees, lifting up handfuls of dry leaves and crumbling them in her hands. The one-o'clock sun, so hot that Lizabeth had worn her denim shorts and thin blue cotton shirt, beat down into the clearing around the house. The air was thick and rich with the heat and the smell of decayed leaves, tree bark, and pine needles over damp earth. Lizabeth's knees felt sticky under her chin.

Beside her, stretched out over the step like a sleeping snake, was a green-handled broom. It was new, with a label still stapled around the bristles. A gray paper sack from Woolworth's lay beside it. Lizabeth had just come from the store. She had raided her piggy

53

bank, which was really a lavender china hippopotamus, and taken out some of the money she'd been saving for their summer holiday. With it she had bought the broom, a picture that she had bought for its oval frame —and that cost much more than she thought she ought to pay—and two squares of flowery material. The material, one piece printed with roses and the other with violets, had come from the remnant table and was half-price. Even the saleslady didn't know what kind it was; probably some sort of synthetic mixture, she said. Lizabeth had hoped it was sprigged muslin because she loved the sound of the words. She decided she would call it that whether it was or not.

Finally Lizabeth decided that she had basked on the steps long enough. The sun was making her sleepy. She stretched lazily, picked up her paper sack and broom, and stood up. After looking around once more to see if the squirrel would appear, she continued up the steps.

The window slipped up easily today, easier than it had before, Lizabeth thought. She pushed the broom through, bristle end first, and let it clatter to the floor. The paper sack she kept in one hand because she didn't want to risk smashing the picture. Then she slipped over the windowsill.

Once in the room, she immediately tore apart the stapled end of the sack and pulled out the squares of material, holding them up before her eyes to admire them. She decided that she liked the violets on the white background much better than the giant red roses on pink, but she was really happy with both. Pressing the material against her cheeks to see how soft it felt, she started toward the rockers, and then suddenly stopped.

The high-backed wicker rocker that had always faced away from the fireplace was now turned towards it. And slowly, it had begun to rock. Lizabeth stood, frozen with terror, her stomach squeezing up inside her like a clenched fist. She wanted to run, but felt as if she had turned to lead, as if everything inside her had stopped.

For a split moment, she thought it might be wind coming through the window and blowing the chair. But there had been no wind outside, and she felt nothing now on her bare legs. The room was hot and still.

Her throat finally loosened a little, and she tried to scream. But it was like pushing wind through a keyhole. Only a tiny squeak came out.

Then a hand appeared on the arm of the rocker.

The sight of it seemed to loosen Lizabeth's own hands. She let go of the material and the paper sack at the same time. As the sack crashed on the floor, there was the sound of splintering glass. At the same moment, Lizabeth finally screamed.

The rocker stopped, and a dark-haired boy stood up. He was not much more than half a head taller than Lizabeth, but his thin wrists hung out a full inch from the sleeves of his torn gray sweatshirt, as if he had recently begun to grow rapidly. He didn't move away from the chair, but stood with his hands pressed to his sides against his jeans, staring at Lizabeth. She knew him. He was Douglas Hunter, Creepy Douglas, C.D.

"I'm sorry," he said simply.

Lizabeth began to sob. They were dry sobs at first that made her chest ache. Then tears began to pour down her face.

"I'm sorry," C.D. repeated. "I'm really sorry. I wouldn't have—I didn't know. Please don't cry."

Lizabeth wiped her wet cheeks on her blouse sleeve, and said nothing.

"I'm sorry," C.D. said again, swallowing hard.

All at once, Lizabeth was filled with a sudden, unreasoning anger. "You creepy class creep! Creep! Creep!" The words poured out of her, sounding sharp and shrill and terrible in the silent house. As soon as she had said them, she gasped, and threw her hands to her mouth.

C.D. looked down, and for a quick, silent moment stood stiffly with his hands pressed hard against his jean legs. Then he raised his eyes directly to Lizabeth. "It's all right. I know my name. I know all of them." It was just a statement of fact. If he'd been angry, he didn't sound it now.

"I'm sorry!" Lizabeth said, and felt her face burning.

"I said it was all right. Forget it. Anyway, it *was* a creepy thing to do, scaring you like that. It was really stupid. Look, are you okay?"

Lizabeth nodded.

"I really am sorry," C.D. said. "When I saw all that stuff on the mantel and art work on the floor, I figured that these little kids had been here and—" He stopped suddenly at the look on Lizabeth's face. "Was it *you* who did it?"

56

Lizabeth started to shake her head, but under C.D.'s steady gaze, she tightened her lips and nodded.

"Oh, boy!" said C.D. "I'm batting a thousand!"

There was an uncomfortable silence between them, but finally C.D. shrugged and said, "I might as well finish the story. These kids I'm talking about are named Morris and Georgie. They're little twerps who infest this neighborhood. Their parents don't like them coming around here, but they come anyway. They'd come more often, but they think the place is haunted. I sort of"—C.D. grinned ruefully—"help the idea along a little. I figured they'd finally found out about the busted latch on that window and come in and done all this. I was sitting on the floor, leaning against the fireplace wall and reading, the way I usually do, when I heard the window open. I flipped the rocker around and got into it just as that broom came floating in. It was stupid! I shouldn't have even tried to scare them the way I did. They could have had a heart attack or something. If that's possible with Morris and Georgie!" He grinned again.

Lizabeth managed a half-smile. Then she dropped her eyes, and they stood again in silence.

"When—when did you first come here?" C.D. asked hesitantly.

"Day before yesterday," Lizabeth replied.

"Alone, like you did today?"

Lizabeth nodded.

"It's funny." C.D. shook his head. "I'd never figure you for someone who'd, well, be interested in a place like this."

57

"Why not?" asked Lizabeth, feeling curiously as if she had to defend herself.

"I don't know. I guess it's because of—those kids you go around with. Besides, I didn't think you were the kind of person who'd dare come climbing into an empty house."

Lizabeth had never considered that all the time the V.I.G.'s and B.'s were watching and making their smart remarks about C.D., he might also be watching and thinking things about them. It startled her, and at the same time it made her feel strangely uncomfortable.

"I'm not—usually," she said.

"Weren't you scared?" C.D. asked.

"I'm not certain," Lizabeth said. "A little, I think."

"I—I come here a lot—mostly to read," C.D. blurted out. He reached down and picked up a paperback book from the rocking chair. "Tolkien," he said. "It's *The Two Towers* from *The Lord of the Rings* trilogy. Have you read any of them?"

Lizabeth thought a moment. "I've read *The Hobbit*. Is that one of them?"

"No, but it does come just before the trilogy. Did you like it?"

"Yes," Lizabeth said.

"Then you ought to read these. I'm—I'm on the second time around," C.D. said, as if he were apologizing for it. He laid the book back on the chair, and there didn't seem to be anything left for either of them to say about the book or about anything else.

Lizabeth shifted uncomfortably. "I guess I ought

to go now." She stooped down for the material and the paper sack that still lay on the floor.

C.D. darted towards her. It was the first time he'd moved from where he stood by the rocking chair. "I'll help you."

Lizabeth didn't want him to help her. She wished he would stay where he was, but before she could say anything, he was already in front of her, leaning over and picking up the paper sack. There was the sharp clink of broken glass.

"What is it? I mean, what *was* it?" C.D. asked.

"A picture."

"Could I buy you another one? It's my fault that it's busted."

"No," Lizabeth said quickly. "No, thank you. I— I won't be needing it anymore."

C.D. handed her the sack, but as she took it from him, he said suddenly, "Do you have to go?"

The question so startled and confused Lizabeth that she could only stare at him blankly.

And she realized then that she had never really looked at C.D. close up like this before. It was the accepted custom of the V.I.G.'s and B.'s to sidle away from C.D. whenever they found themselves near him. Lizabeth, who was almost always with one or another of the group, had always moved away with them. She hadn't really thought much about it. It was simply something you did.

Now she was so close she could see the lump in his throat rise and fall as he breathed. She saw the fine, pale sprinkling of freckles across his nose, and the tiny chip in his left front tooth. He smelled as if he had just bathed with Ivory soap. For some reason, this surprised Lizabeth. Perhaps it was because she thought someone like C.D. ought not to smell like Ivory soap.

His eyes, looking at her questioningly, were direct and steady, and the deepest blue Lizabeth had ever seen. The look, as well as the color of them, was strangely disconcerting. The funny thought came to Lizabeth that Sharon would have been jealous of C.D.'s thick, long lashes, if she had ever noticed them.

Still, he was C.D., Creepy Douglas, and no matter how his eyes looked, she wasn't certain she wanted to remain in the house with him. In confusion, she dropped her eyes.

"You don't have to leave," C.D. said quickly. "I'll go and you can stay." It was as if he had read her mind.

Lizabeth felt her cheeks burning again. "But it's your house!" she burst out. "I mean, you were here first."

"It—it belongs to whoever's here," C.D. said at once. "Look, why don't you stay and do whatever you came to do. I'll go on reading. I won't bother you."

Lizabeth hesitated. "Well, I was only going to clean. I got the broom today, and I brought some things yesterday in that sack." She pointed toward the fireplace.

C.D. crossed the room and was back in a moment with the sack in his hand. "You know, I never even saw it. I must be losing my eyesight. Here." He handed Lizabeth the sack and started toward the fireplace. "I'll get back to my book. Have fun!" He flopped on the floor and seemed to lose himself in his book immediately.

Lizabeth felt as if she had been caught in a trap, but there was no polite way out of it. Wishing that she had been able to think of something quickly, like a dentist appointment, she could do nothing now but take out the bottle of window cleaner and a handful of paper towels and go to work. But all the time she was rubbing on the windows across the room from C.D., she felt as if she were putting on a performance in a cage. She was certain C.D. must be staring at her, and yet whenever she stole a look at him over her shoulder, his head was bent over his book as if she weren't even in the room. Still, she felt stiff and burning hot just knowing that he was sitting behind her. She wondered stupidly if her *legs* were blushing.

The minutes passed slowly by. But then, just as it often happened with Lizabeth when she was doing something that interested her, she became engrossed in the job of window cleaning. She had never before worked on anything so dirty as these windows, and it fascinated her to see the film of grease and dirt vanish with the magical help of the liquid in the bottle. But she was disappointed to find that she could reach only the lower two-thirds of the windows. She contented herself with that until she came to the fourth window, and then decided that perhaps she hadn't tried hard enough. She stood on her tiptoes, stretching upward as far as she possibly could, and gave a small sigh of annoyance.

"Can I help?" C.D. asked.

The sound of his voice startled Lizabeth. He had been so quiet, and she had become so deep in her work, that she had almost forgotten he was there.

"It's nothing," she said. "I just can't reach the tops of the windows. They're too high."

"Maybe I can do it. I have pretty long arms." C. D. dropped his book, jumped up, and came towards her. "Would you like me to try?"

Lizabeth had no choice but to say, "Thank you," and hand him a paper towel and the bottle of cleaner. A moment later, the top of the window was as clean as the rest of it.

"Okay?" said C.D.

"Okay," said Lizabeth, and smiled.

"I might as well finish up the rest of them," C.D. said. "You can go on with the others."

He went right to work, and Lizabeth moved to the window on the other side of the door. She wasn't certain whether or not she liked the idea of C.D. helping her, but she decided finally that it was pleasanter than having him sit on the floor behind her. Even though they weren't talking, the silence wasn't such an uncomfortable one.

"Oh!" Lizabeth cried out suddenly.

"What is it?" C.D. said. "Did you hurt yourself?"

"Oh, no," Lizabeth replied promptly. "It's the squirrel. I was waiting for him before I came into the house. Now he's finally arrived. He's on the railing." She pressed her nose against the window.

C.D. laughed. "Oh, that's only old Nutsy. He never stays away long."

"Nutsy?" said Lizabeth curiously.

C.D. looked embarrassed. "I just named him after this squirrel in a—well, in a little kids' book." He began to redden. "It's kind of stupid, I guess."

"You don't mean Squirrel Nutkin from Beatrix Potter, do you?"

"Yeah, that's the one," said C.D., his eyes widening. "How'd you guess?"

"Because I named him the very same thing," replied Lizabeth, rather indignantly. "Well, I called him Squirrel Nutkin anyway."

"No kidding?"

"No kidding," said Lizabeth. "Besides, I don't think anything from Beatrix Potter is stupid."

"I don't either, but you have to say it to protect yourself!"

"I know," Lizabeth said. She thought of the way she had to hide her dolls each time Sharon came to visit.

When they finally went back to polishing windows, Lizabeth began to hum.

"I guess you've explored the house, haven't you?" C.D. asked over his shoulder.

"No, not yet."

"No kidding?"

"No kidding," said Lizabeth, and suddenly, they were both laughing.

"Would you like to go through now?" C.D. asked.

"I—I guess so."

C.D. dropped his paper towel. "Come on then! We can do this later." He ran toward the wide doorway with the open glass doors, and Lizabeth followed him.

They went from room to room, with C.D. giving a running commentary in each one. After going through what was probably the dining room beyond the glass doors, they went into what C.D. said was a bedroom, though it was so tiny that Lizabeth was certain it was only a closet. But C.D. opened a door to show her what *was* the closet, and then had her peer into the bathroom. In it crouched a huge, claw-footed, rusty old bathtub that looked like a scaly beast waiting for its prey.

"Ugh!" said Lizabeth.

"I agree," said C.D. cheerfully.

They went to the kitchen. Shadowed by tall trees that hung over its windows like witches' capes, it turned out to be dark and gloomy as Lizabeth had suspected. She was glad she hadn't come there alone for the first time.

"It doesn't smell very nice," she said, wrinkling her nose.

"It smells terrible! It could use a good bath." C.D. peered into the sink. "Two empty beer cans. Why is it everyplace you go, you always find two empty beer cans."

"Or an empty Coke bottle," said Lizabeth.

"Let's go upstairs," C.D. said.

On their way from the kitchen, he opened a door that looked as if it were the entrance to an underground cave. "The cellar," he announced. "You don't want to go into the cellar, do you?"

Lizabeth shook her head firmly. "There might be rats!"

"There might be," C.D. said matter-of-factly, and shut the door.

They clattered up the stairs to the second floor.

After exploring the two small rooms at the back and side of the house, some closets, and a bathroom that they both agreed was papered in a rare shade of throw-up pink, they came to another large, sunlit room at the front of the house.

"With a fireplace and everything," C.D. said. "It's just as nice as the room below it—nicer, maybe. Come over and look." He walked to one of the windows, and Lizabeth followed.

She found that she was looking across the faded green-shingled roof of the veranda in a view that skimmed the tops of the trees to something that glistened way in the distance.

"It's beautiful!" she breathed. "Is that the river?"

"I think so, but I'm not sure. Sometimes I think it's only the sky."

"It's the river," Lizabeth said in a positive voice.

"Yes, ma'am!" C.D. said with a grin. He pointed a stiff finger at the window. "Lizabeth Bracken says you are a river. *Be* a river!"

Lizabeth laughed, but at the same time thought how strange it sounded to hear C.D. saying her name, to think that he even knew it at all. Could she really have thought that he sat in class never seeing anything, never thinking anything? She supposed she had, if she thought about it at all. It seemed curious now.

She realized that she hadn't yet addressed C.D. by any name. How long, she wondered, could you know someone and never call them anything? Perhaps in this case it didn't matter. Perhaps this was the last time she would ever be talking with C.D.

"Look!" he cried suddenly. "Did you see that?"

"What?"

"That little brown bush twitching at the corner of the veranda roof."

"Nutsy!" exclaimed Lizabeth. "I didn't know he came up here."

"He practically lives up here," C.D. said. "He stores stuff in that drainpipe when he thinks no one sees him. Watch."

The squirrel's nose and bright black eyes appeared over the edge of the roof. Apparently satisfied that he was not being seen, he raced across the shingles, his tail in the air like a feather duster. After rummaging around in the leaves of the drainpipe at the corner of the roof, he sat for a moment, carelessly twitching his tail. Then he leaped over the side of the roof and disappeared.

Lizabeth laughed until tears came to her eyes. Still laughing, she looked at her watch. "Oh! I really have to go now."

C.D. turned towards her with a sharp look of disappointment in his eyes. But he smiled and said, "Okay," without asking any questions.

But back downstairs, as Lizabeth was gathering up

the things she'd brought, he said suddenly, "Hey! You can leave your stuff here if you like. I'm the only one who comes in this house, I think. No one's going to take anything."

Lizabeth wasn't worried about anything being taken. The truth was that she wasn't certain if she was coming back to the house. After all, Sharon had once told her that you might as well be dead as caught having anything to do with C.D. No matter how she might have acted that afternoon, the thought had never once left her mind that this was Creepy Douglas.

"Well—all right," she said, letting the two pieces of material fall into a limp heap on the wooden rocker. She wondered if she would ever see them again.

With a kind of grateful half-smile, C.D. pushed open the window for her. She began climbing out, and then turned toward him. "I'll see you—I'll see you—" she faltered, and ended limply, "in school, I guess."

It would have been better if she'd said nothing at all. The hesitation was exactly long enough to let C.D. know what it meant.

C.D.'s mouth seemed still to be smiling, but all expression had suddenly left his eyes. "Yeah, sure," he said, staring at the windowsill.

Lizabeth found that she was trembling as she walked up the path toward the street, but then she knew there was nothing she could do about it, really nothing. She hoped C.D. wouldn't take advantage in school of their accidentally having spent a few moments together in an old house.

Chapter 6

ON MONDAY MORNING, Lizabeth discovered that she had nothing to worry about. She was standing next to Dennis Stickley and Hank McGinnis and some others, listening to Mrs. Poole explain a difficult math problem they'd had for homework, when she saw Dennis spear Hank in the ribs with a well-practiced finger.

"Ouch! Cut it out!" said Hank under his breath.

"Shut up and look who's coming," hissed Dennis. "Watch me get him."

"You can't here," Hank whispered. "He'll squeal."

"He wouldn't dare," said Dennis.

Lizabeth turned quickly and saw C.D. coming toward them. But almost as soon as she did, he wheeled around and went back to his desk.

"Changed his mind. Nuts!" Dennis scowled. "Wonder what got into him?"

Hank grinned. "He must have seen your beautiful face!"

Lizabeth was certain, though, that he'd returned to his desk because he had seen *her*. During the day, she became more sure of it than ever. He seemed to be trying to keep as far away from her as possible, even if it meant detouring all around the room to do it. It became increasingly clear that she wasn't going to have any problems because of the meeting at the house. It was a relief, but at the same time, it caused a heavy, uneasy lump inside her that wouldn't go away. C.D. was no longer just an object in the classroom now. He was a person. Lizabeth knew that she must have hurt him, and she didn't like hurting anyone, even C.D. She was uncomfortably aware of his presence all day.

Still, she had no intention of doing anything about it. And she knew that she could never return to the house. She could not risk meeting him there again.

Though she was never quite successful in trying to forget the house, she was at least able to stay away from it. She took her short way to and from school every day so she wouldn't go near it, and she was helped in staying away by keeping busy almost every afternoon with the Pop-Pop Girls. For four straight days, they met at one or another of their homes to pop and string corn, try on their dresses, or rehearse their singing and dancing. Then on Friday, because there was no school the next day, they decided to meet at Sharon's house that night instead of meeting in the afternoon.

Every day that week, Mrs. Poole had given the class a free period to work on the variety show. Everyone met with their respective groups either in the classroom or in some empty room in the school. The Pop-

Pop Girls went to the cafeteria. Whether it was because this was the last period of the week or simply because they'd been working too long on the act, no one knew, but the Friday rehearsal was a near-disaster. They didn't accomplish anything.

Dody kept accusing Betsy of being out of step. They had a terrible row about it, and for a few minutes Betsy refused to go on rehearsing. Sharon and Martha were both in a grumpy mood. But when Lizabeth hesitantly suggested that perhaps they needed a holiday from rehearsing, all four of them snapped at her. Sharon acted very sniffy towards her at the end of the day, and she left school close to tears.

Head bent low over her books, she hurried from the crowded playground to the street. She didn't want to meet or talk with anyone. But the street seemed as crowded as the playground. A large gang of fifth graders were walking directly ahead of her, all carrying packages tied with bright ribbons. Although they seemed to be on their way to someone's birthday party, they dawdled around as if they weren't going anyplace at all. To keep from having to make her way through them, Lizabeth turned off at the first street she came to, and it was the street she had carefully avoided all week. But she didn't really care. She had known all along that one way or another, she would find the excuse to be there. She didn't hesitate a moment when she came to the worn brick path, but turned right into it.

The crunching, creaking sounds of her feet on the stair treads going up to the veranda were comfortingly familiar, like the ticking of a nursery clock at night. The

pungent, welcoming smells of earth and dry leaves and the old wood of the house rushed to greet her. Still, Lizabeth's heart thumped in her chest like a toy drum as she walked slowly up the steps.

Each time she had come before, she had known the house was empty, or at least thought it was. It was an entirely different feeling, thinking there might be someone inside, someone she didn't want to meet.

What would she do if *he* was there? Lizabeth asked herself. Well, she would very politely say that she needed her things and had come to get them. Then, without getting into further conversations about the squirrel, books, or even the house itself, she would gather everything up and leave. It ought to be very simple, and there was nothing to be nervous about. But Lizabeth couldn't keep her heart from jumping into her throat as she wiped a spot on the window and peered through it. She took a deep breath when she saw that the room was empty. Quickly laying her books on the floor, she lifted the window and clambered through.

The tall wicker rocker faced the window once more, but outside of that, nothing in the room had been touched since she'd left it. Crumpled pieces of paper towel lay on the floor and windowsills where she and C.D. had dropped them when they went to explore the house. The broom was stretched out by the glass doors where it had toppled over, and the material still lay in untidy heaps of violet and rose where Lizabeth had thrown them. Her gifts to the house still reached forlornly across the mantel. By now the pine needles had begun to look sad and gray.

Lizabeth stared around the room, not knowing what to make of it. It was as if C.D. had left the house, just as she had, and never come back to it. It was as if he had—left the house to *her!* The thought left Lizabeth with an odd blank feeling. Why, she wondered, wasn't she thrilled and relieved about it? Wasn't that exactly what she wanted?

She picked up a paper towel and began to rub it listlessly over a window. The house seemed so still and quiet. She had liked that before, but now it only made the house feel empty. She wondered what was the matter with her.

And then suddenly, she knew. She had just discovered in her deepest thoughts, the ones she often never admitted even to herself, that she had really wanted to find C.D. there when she came into the house. She had probably wanted it all along.

The next day Lizabeth returned to the house, and there was still no sign that C.D. had been there. But she decided that she would not think about it and would go right on with all the things she had planned for the house to start with. She dusted the windowsills. She swept the floor. She folded the material and laid it on the seats of the rocking chairs. They were only an excuse for pillows, but the violets and roses brightened the room. Someday she would make the material up into real pillows, Lizabeth told herself.

Finally, she took her Woolworth's picture from its paper sack, carefully lifted off the sharp, ugly shards of broken glass, and hung it by the fireplace on a nail left from a former picture. Lizabeth wondered now why she had invested so much of her savings from her hippopotamus bank in the picture, even if it did have a pretty oval frame. It was a terrible printed landscape with mountains, trees, a stream, a lake, and huge, billowing clouds, all in wildly improbable electric colors. She wondered what C.D. would have said about it if he'd seen it.

It came to her that no matter what she did, she couldn't help thinking about C.D.—when she saw Nutsy on the veranda railing, when she ran upstairs to look out the window, when she tried out the wicker rocking chair and discovered that it wobbled dangerously. She hadn't known it took such courage to sit in it! And all the time she was working, she kept hoping that he'd decide to come back to the house. But he never did.

Was he ever coming back to the house? Lizabeth wondered. And if he did, how would she know it? Before she left that afternoon, she found three tiny pebbles and laid them on the windowsill, so anyone coming in or out the window would easily brush against them. That way she would find out what she wanted to know.

Lizabeth always spent Sundays with her family, so it was Monday morning on the way to school before she could check on the pebbles. She found them lying there exactly as she'd left them. They were still there on the following Saturday afternoon, one week later. And all that week, C.D. continued to keep away from her at school.

Perhaps it was just as well, Lizabeth told herself, especially when she was with the V.I.G.'s. That one bad afternoon aside, they were having a marvelous time getting ready for the variety show. The Pop-Pop Girls seemed to be the queen bees and the envy of everyone. So she had the house, and the V.I.G.'s and B.'s as well. Why should she complicate her life with C.D.? Lizabeth wondered.

But when she dropped over the sill into the house, it was as if she had a spell cast upon her. The school Lizabeth became the house Lizabeth, two different people, wanting two different things. Inside the house, Lizabeth knew that she still wanted C.D. to come back. Would he, even if he knew that she wanted him to? He had every right to hate her now. Did he? How did one go about finding out something like that?

With the variety show set for Wednesday night, there was to be a dress rehearsal Monday night, so the Pop-Pop girls decided not to meet Monday afternoon. Early Monday morning, Lizabeth got out of bed, and went to her desk. She pulled a piece of notebook paper from her school folder, and then wrote:

Nutsy says that he wishes you would come back to the house. He will try to be there this afternoon after school.

Lizabeth

During lunch hour, Lizabeth slipped away from the cafeteria and returned to the classroom. She found it empty. C.D.'s book, *The Two Towers,* lay on his desk with a slip of paper in it marking where he'd left off reading. Lizabeth removed the paper and replaced it with her note.

When she arrived at the house after school, the pebbles were missing from the windowsill. A stack of school books lay on the veranda floor under it. On top was a worn paperback copy of *The Two Towers*.

Chapter 7

C.D. JUMPED UP from the floor by the fireplace as soon as Lizabeth slipped through the open window and stood before it. They looked across the room at one another with questioning eyes, not smiling.

"Hi," C.D. said.

"Hi," said Lizabeth.

The room was terribly still.

C.D. motioned across the fireplace with one hand. "Have a seat." He dropped to the floor again and drew up his knees, resting his elbows on them. In silence, he watched Lizabeth cross the room. As soon as she sat down, he lowered his eyes and sat curling the lace from a black sneaker around one finger.

Lizabeth folded her legs under her, clasped her hands in her lap, and sat memorizing the cracks in the brick hearth in front of her.

"What—what should I call you?" she asked.

"My family calls me Loren. My father and I were both Douglas Loren Hunter, but he was Doug. You can call me Loren if you like."

"Loren," Lizabeth said. "That's a nice name."

"It's a name," Loren said. "It's okay."

A droning plane far above them helped fill the silence for a moment.

"The room looks nice. You did some stuff to it," Loren said. His eyes remained fixed on his sneaker lace.

"Not very much," Lizabeth said. She completed her study of the hearth and concentrated on the blue polka dots in her cotton skirt. "I just swept a little. I hung the picture, too."

"I noticed," Loren said. "It's—it's very pretty."

At this, Lizabeth's eyes flew open, and she looked up. She found Loren looking back at her with a puzzled expression. There was a moment's hesitation; then his eyes began to twinkle. "If you want to know, it's ghoulish. It really stinks!"

Lizabeth smiled. "I *thought* you'd like it."

"Heck, I didn't know," Loren said. "I thought maybe you'd actually paid real live money for it."

"I did in a way," Lizabeth told him. "It came with the frame."

Suddenly, Loren jumped up and pressed his nose against the picture. "You know, the closer you get, the worse it looks. The colors aren't even printed inside the lines. Hey, you know something?"

"What?"

"It's really a terrible picture!"

"Well, I *am* going to change it," Lizabeth said defensively.

"No, don't!" Loren thumped back down on the floor. "I mean, I don't think you should."

"Why not?" Lizabeth asked, surprised.

"I don't know. I can't really explain it. It just seems to go with the house."

"I think I know what you mean," Lizabeth said. "All right then, we'll—we'll keep it!"

Their eyes met for a moment, but neither one said anything. Lizabeth had used the word *we,* and Loren had heard it. The meaning of it left them with too much to say, so they could say nothing.

Then all at once, Loren began to fish around in his jeans pocket and pulled out what looked like a small, crumpled ball of tinfoil and yellow paper. He gazed at it ruefully. "I found this in my pocket just before you came in. Two lemon Lifesavers. I think they went through the wash with my jeans. Would you like one?"

Lizabeth held out her hand, and Loren put one in it.

"I think you're right. It's pretty sticky," she said, and popped it into her mouth. A moment later, her tongue firmly implanted in the hole of the Lifesaver, she lisped, "Does your tongue sting when you put it through the middle?"

"Yes, especially on lemon and orange," Loren lisped back.

"I wonder why we do it then?" asked Lizabeth.

Loren grinned. "Because it's there!"

Sucking on their candy, they fell into another silence, a comfortable one this time. It was as if they had suddenly crossed a huge hurdle. A conversation was necessary only if they felt like having one.

Loren stretched out his long, thin legs and leaned back on his hands. "Hey, you know something else?"

"What?" asked Lizabeth.

"You've never told me how you first came here."

"I just came by one day on the way from school," Lizabeth replied carelessly.

"Is that all? You just decided to drop in one day for no reason?"

Lizabeth hesitated. "Well, not exactly."

"Oh," Loren said. "Look, you don't have to tell me about it. So you just came by one day on the way home from school. That's good enough for me."

Lizabeth returned to studying the polka dots on her skirt. "I'd like to tell you," she said softly.

Sitting across from this dark-haired boy who was almost a stranger, the sixth-grade outcast, in an old, deserted, cast-off house, Lizabeth was surprised at how easy it was to tell the story of how she came to be there. She could tell about the summer house, about how she had cried that morning and had such a bad time with Sharon, about how, finally, she had come down the path to the house, accidentally found that the window would open, and then climbed through it.

"I drew the stick people that day," Lizabeth said. "The next morning before school I came back and put the things on the mantel. It seemed like a kind of magic spell then."

Loren winced. "That was some magic spell. The next time you came back, you found me! You'd better quit with the magic spells."

Lizabeth laughed.

"Why didn't you tell Sharon about not going to the summer house?" Loren asked. "Does she bite or something?"

"I couldn't tell her," Lizabeth said. "She's never understood about things like the summer house, so she certainly wouldn't understand about *this* house."

"You mean she doesn't know about it either?"

Lizabeth shook her head. "No, nobody knows about it. It's—it's my secret house."

A strange look crossed Loren's face. He dropped his eyes, almost as if he were trying to hide them, but he raised them again quickly and said, "It's my secret house too." Then, in the very next breath, he added, "Hey! Let's rock!"

Lizabeth looked at him in surprise.

"I meant on the rocking chairs!" Loren jumped up, laughing.

Lizabeth drew her arms around herself and shuddered. "I've tried the wicker one. It's pretty spooky."

"I know," said Loren with a wide grin. "I'll take it. You may have the safe one, ma'am!" He let himself down gingerly onto the rocker as if he expected it to explode. It only gave a pained squeak.

Safely settled on the sturdy wooden rocker, Lizabeth giggled.

"You know," Loren said. "When I was a kid, the back leg of my rocking horse got busted. I tried to fix

81

it, but somehow I knocked an inch off the leg. I nearly got seasick riding that old horse, and this chair rocks just like it did. Listen to that death rattle! Sounds like it's going to go any minute." Suddenly, he began to speed up the pace of the rocker. "Let's race!"

Laughing, they both began to go faster and faster, until all at once Lizabeth somehow let go of the arms and went catapulting out of her rocker.

Loren quickly brought his rocking chair to a groaning, creaking stop. "Are you okay?" he asked anxiously.

Lizabeth was giggling so hard she could barely nod her head. "I—I thought you said that chair was s-s-s-safe!"

Loren shook his head gravely. "Only if you stay in it, ma'am. As for the race, I am forced to declare a tie. You went farther, but *I* remained in the saddle!"

The ridiculous grin that followed the solemn look on Loren's face seemed so funny to Lizabeth that she collapsed on the floor, choking with laughter. It was minutes before she was able to catch her breath enough to say, "Could we explore the house again?"

They went through the house, discovering new things, finding new things to say about what they had seen before.

"Listen," Loren said, turning on the iron faucet over the kitchen sink.

Lizabeth tilted her head and concentrated. "I don't hear anything."

"Exactly! Doesn't it make you feel funny, turning on a faucet and not having something happen?"

"It makes you feel funny turning on anything and

82

not having something happen," Lizabeth said. "Like a stove or an iron or a television set."

"Or a light bulb," Loren added. He reached out and pulled the string hanging from a bare bulb over the sink. "Think how once it must have seemed like magic to push a button or pull a string and have a light come on, or have anything happen at all."

"Now this house seems like magic because nothing like that *does* happen," Lizabeth said, staring dreamily at the dusty, lifeless gray bulb.

"Maybe it really is," Loren said.

Next, they ran upstairs to look out the windows and to see if Nutsy might appear on the veranda roof. After a long wait and no sign of the squirrel, they thumped back down again and settled themselves in front of the fireplace. A few moments of quiet passed; then Loren picked a dust ball from the hearth and blew it thoughtfully off one finger.

"Lizabeth?"

"What?"

"You've never said so exactly, but were you trying to make this house be like the summer house you couldn't go to? I mean, bringing all that stuff here and everything."

Lizabeth looked at Loren quickly to see if he might be laughing at her, but he wasn't. "I'm not certain, but I think so. I was going to find lots of old things" —she looked sideways at the picture hanging by the fireplace chimney—"make-believe old, anyway. I guess it was a crazy idea."

"I don't think it's such a crazy idea. You can still

try to do it. Correction, *we* can still try." Loren gave an uncertain little laugh. "I mean, I'd like to help if you want me to."

"Oh, yes!" Lizabeth said. "I really would! We could begin planning right now if you'd like."

"I'd like!" Loren said. He jumped up, beaming. "Look, don't go away. I'm going to get something."

His long legs covered the distance to the window in a few swift steps. He leaned out and was back in a moment, waving a notebook and pencil in the air. "I left all my stuff out there so you wouldn't come in and get scared half to death again."

"I thought you did," Lizabeth said. "I left my books out there, too, because it's easier than carrying them through the window. Do you think we should?"

"Oh heck, no one ever—" Loren stopped. His eyebrows flew up. "Morris and Georgie! Maybe I'd *better* bring them in.

"You know what?" he said as he lifted in their two stacks of books. "Maybe we ought to have some kind of secret sign when one of us is in the house. Nothing that sticks out like a sore thumb, though, like school books."

Without thinking, Lizabeth said eagerly, "We could leave little pebbles on the windowsill!"

Loren looked at her sharply, and then smiled. "Was that you who put those things there? I wondered about that."

Lizabeth felt herself blushing furiously. "I—I didn't know how to find out if you'd ever come back to the house. I thought that—" she faltered and stopped in confusion.

84

"Hey, please don't be embarrassed," Loren said quickly. "Heck, I'm really flattered. I mean it! Anyway, I think the pebbles are a great idea. Pebbles on the windowsill—sounds like the title of a mystery." He smiled at Lizabeth. "It's okay with me. Okay with you, too?"

"Okay with me," said Lizabeth.

Loren sat down by the fireplace and spread the notebook across his legs. "Let's get to work!"

"Let's!" said Lizabeth happily.

Furnishing the house, she said a while later, was certainly going to take a lot of thought.

"It will have to," Loren commented wryly. "There isn't going to be a lot of cash around. At least, I don't have much until I start my lawn-mowing jobs later. You aren't by any chance a millionairess, are you?"

Lizabeth sighed. "No! I have a bank account I'm not allowed to touch, and a half-full piggy bank. It's really a hippopotamus," she explained, in case it made a difference.

"Assets," said Loren, writing in his notebook. "Lizabeth Bracken's half-full hippopotamus bank, Loren Hunter's three-quarter empty piggy bank—and brains." Chewing his pencil eraser, he studied what he'd written.

"Maybe we'd better do just one room," Lizabeth said. "Just *this* one."

"Maybe we don't have a choice," Loren said, and grinned. Then his eyes wandered over the windows that ran across the front of the house. "But not this room—better do the room *over* it," he added thoughtfully.

"Why?" Lizabeth asked. This was the first room she'd come into. It was the room where she had hung her first picture and covered her first chairs. She wanted to stay in it.

"Morris and Georgie," said Loren flatly. "If they ever look through those windows and find out something's going on—pow!"

"Well . . ." Lizabeth hesitated.

"There's a fireplace up there, just like down here," said Loren.

Lizabeth sighed.

"And a view. You can see over the treetops." Loren looked at her hopefully.

Lizabeth finally smiled and nodded. "All right, you win. And I guess as long as we're moving, we might as well do it right away."

Loren returned her smile. "Yep! The sooner the better where those two characters are concerned."

"Haven't they ever found out they could come through the window if they wanted to?" Lizabeth asked.

"Nope," said Loren. "I think they really would tell me if they had. Believe it or not, I'm their good friend. Which is why I keep letting them know the house is haunted. Got to protect little kids like that."

Lizabeth stood up and dusted off her skirt. "I wonder how the latch got broken in the first place? The door is locked, and so is everything else, isn't it?" She looked questioningly at Loren and was surprised by the strange look that she saw suddenly in his eyes.

He leaned over, and with a quick, jerky motion,

picked up the broom. "Beats me. Hey, let's get going!"

"All right," said Lizabeth. She only wondered for a moment why Loren was so startled by her question, and then forgot all about it.

She started to pick up the pinecones from the mantel, and then stopped, biting her lip. She'd just remembered what Loren had said that first day, about how he thought little kids had brought in all the things. "I guess we don't have to take this silly stuff up," she blurted out. "We can throw it away."

"It's not silly," Loren said firmly. "It's like the picture. It goes with the house. Anyway," he added with a grin, "maybe it really is a spell! We can't risk throwing it away. We'll take it all up, except for those people on the floor. We can't—hey, I just noticed! What happened to them?"

"I accidentally swept them away," said Lizabeth.

"That's a disaster! A real loss to the art world!" Loren shook his head mournfully.

Lizabeth giggled.

A few minutes later, except for brighter windows, the downstairs front room looked just as it had when Lizabeth first stepped into it. The mantel was empty. The picture had left the wall. The bright spots of color made by the violets and roses in Lizabeth's pieces of "sprigged muslin" were gone. All that was left were the stiff lace curtains on the windows, and the two rocking chairs staring blankly at one another in the middle of the floor.

Upstairs, it was only a short while before Loren had swept out the room, and Lizabeth had decorated the mantel with the pinecones, the acorn cups, the egg-shaped pink rock, and even the pine branches, though they were now brown and brittle as straw. The oval picture now rested complacently on its nail by the fireplace, and the roses and violets lay in bright, neat squares on either side of the hearth like tidy little flower gardens.

"But the room looks so empty," Lizabeth wailed. "I wish we could have brought up the rocking chairs, too."

"We couldn't," Loren said. "*You* know—"

"Morris and Georgie!" Lizabeth said it with him.

Loren grinned. "You're learning fast. Hey, don't look so sad. The room won't stay empty for long. Let's get back to work on it."

They settled down once more beside the fireplace, the squares of material serving as pillows, and Loren spread his notebook across his knees.

The sun was making long, sharp angles with the floor before Lizabeth thought about looking at her watch.

When she saw the time, she gasped. "Loren, it's past five o'clock! But we haven't *done* anything!"

Loren scratched his ear and shook his head ruefully as he looked down at a page only one-quarter filled in his notebook. "Well, we talked a lot."

They looked at one another and grinned. What Loren had said was true, and though they'd talked a lot, it wasn't about the house.

"But what *did* we talk about?" said Lizabeth.

"Who knows?" Loren shrugged. "Shoes and ships and sealing wax, I guess."

"And cabbages and kings," said Lizabeth. And then counting on her fingers, she added, "And our families and my friend Janey in California and the Winston Towers, ugh!" She paused to wrinkle her nose. "And pictures and television shows and Mickey Mouse watches and *Winnie-the-Pooh* and *The Wind in the Willows* and pizza pies and—"

"Pizza pies?" interrupted Loren. "How did they get in there?"

"You said it was your favorite food."

"I did?"

"Oh, Loren!" Lizabeth tried, but not very successfully, to look disgusted with him.

"Okay," he said blandly, "go on. Pizza pies and . . ."

"Loren, I really do have to go!" Lizabeth clambered to her feet, laughing.

Loren folded his notebook, stretched his long legs, and hoisted himself up. "Hey, when are you coming back?"

Lizabeth looked down on the pattern of cloth violets at her feet and wondered why she felt so shy. "I have things to do every afternoon this week. I—I guess Saturday afternoon." Then suddenly she knew that she was thinking—and what about all the days between now and then, Lizabeth Elvira Bracken? What about them?

But she couldn't stand there staring at cloth violets forever. She looked up and saw that the laughter in Loren's eyes had disappeared. They stared at one another helplessly for a moment. Then Lizabeth dropped her eyes again, and Loren said evenly, "Look, there is one thing we didn't talk about. I guess you know what that is."

Slowly Lizabeth nodded.

"School," Loren said.

Lizabeth felt her lips trembling. "But I—I don't care! I—"

"Yes, you *do* care." Loren broke in in a steady voice. "And I happen to care too. So we're just going to be friends here, and not in school. Okay?"

Lizabeth shook her head. Loren stared at her for a moment, then wheeled around and went to the window. His back towards her, he began to talk quietly. "There was this new guy at the beginning of the year." He turned to face Lizabeth again. "His name is Bill Potter. He's a pretty nice guy, and we started being friends. Then Dennis Stickley and—and some of those other guys found out about it and began going after Bill."

"Isn't Bill Potter in Mrs. Nickerson's class?" Lizabeth asked.

Loren nodded. "His folks got him moved out of Mrs. Poole's class. Now all we do is say 'hi' in the hallway. Look!" Loren smiled at her. "You said this was your secret house. So I can be your secret friend. Okay?"

No, Lizabeth thought, of course it wasn't okay! How could it be? How would she feel if someone kept her a secret because he didn't dare admit she was his friend? But in the beginning, all she had wanted was another friend like Janey. She had never asked to have a complicated friend like Loren. Now he was giving her a way out of the trap, so shouldn't she take it?

Secret house! Secret friend! Secret summer! What was wrong with that? "Okay," Lizabeth said. But the smile she gave Loren was a hesitant, uncertain smile.

Chapter 8

"Rooty-toot-toot! Rooty-toot-toot!
We are the girls from the Institute!
We don't smoke, and we don't chew,
And we don't go with the boys who do!"

DODY GREEN chanted the words as she pranced in front
of Sharon's long closet mirror, her hands on her hips.
Flapping one-inch-long artificial lashes over her eyes,
she studied her reflection lovingly, then looked hopefully over her shoulder to see if anyone was paying any
attention to her.

All five Pop-Pop Girls, plus Lynda Eberhard,
Sharon's sister who was a junior in high school, and
Mrs. Eberhard, were packed into Sharon's tiny second-
floor bedroom, where the girls were getting dressed for
the variety show. A pale green slip hung drunkenly over
the desk lamp. Shorts, blouses, purses, lipstick-stained

towels, and socks lay strewn over the pink chenille bed-spread like the remnants of a wild rummage sale. Nobody bothered to move a pile of shoes dumped in the middle of the floor. They stepped over or around them as if they weren't even there. The warm, damp room was solidly filled with the smells of hair spray, liquid makeup, and somebody's mother's Tigress cologne.

"Did you really make those words up?" Martha Cambridge asked Dody. She was sitting stiffly on the edge of Sharon's bed as Lynda Eberhard attempted, with not too much success, to pin up her long hair.

"Maybe I did, and maybe I didn't," said Dody, flirting with herself in the mirror.

"She didn't," said Sharon from in front of her dresser where, with a shaky hand, she was applying a ring of black eye makeup around Lizabeth's eyes. The ring was growing thicker by the second. "Did she, Mother?" Sharon asked.

Mrs. Eberhard's mouth was an arsenal of bristling pins as she sat on the floor under Betsy Farrell's skirt, trying to repair the damage to the hem made when Betsy tried to pull her dress over giant metal hair curlers. All she could manage to do was grunt something that sounded like "yes."

"There, you see!" said Sharon.

"It's funny anyway, Dody," Lizabeth offered helpfully, turning her head a fraction of an inch.

The brush in Sharon's hand quivered up at one corner of Lizabeth's eye. "Oh, Lizabeth!" she shrieked. "See what you've made me do. Now I have to match the other side."

"I'm sorry," said Lizabeth. Her eyes already looked as if she were recovering from a long siege of malaria. She couldn't see where a little more black made any difference.

Mrs. Eberhard removed the pins from her mouth and dropped them into a plastic sewing box by her feet. "I remember that from when I was in school," she said, nodding her head happily, as if the subject of Dody's recitation was still in progress. Then, with the smoothness of long practice, she raised the tone of her voice two octaves without drawing a breath and bellowed, "Will you two leave the room? Now, I don't want to have to speak to you again!" After that, she went calmly back to rummaging in her sewing box for needle and thread.

Ever since the girls had opened the bedroom door to let in some air, Sharon's seven-year-old twin brothers had been hanging around the doorway with their jaws gaping open, taking in as much as they could. When they found no one seemed to be noticing them, they sidled all the way into the room. They had been ordered away twice before, but each time had returned to haunt the doorway. Now, after an apparent detour to the kitchen, they were back in the room with mouths framed in sticky rings of chocolate, spilling crumbs from giant sugar cookies all over the floor, and staring. At their mother's command, they straggled out a third time without a word. But a part of one of the twins, munching on his cookies, was still reflected in the dresser mirror, showing that the two boys had only gone into hiding behind the door frame.

"Oh, honestly!" Sharon said. "Will somebody please shut the door!"

"If we do, we'll suffocate," said Betsy.

"We can open the window," Sharon shot back.

Martha sniffed ominously. "You can't. I'll start my hay fever."

"Oh, honestly, *Mother!*" said Sharon.

Mrs. Eberhard hoisted herself up from the floor and stamped to the door. There was the sound of four resounding swats from the hallway, two for each twin, followed by their piercing shrieks as they fled down the stairs. With no expression on her face, Mrs. Eberhard returned to Betsy and lowered herself to the floor with a soft sigh.

Lizabeth remembered the first time she had ever met Mrs. Eberhard. She had somehow expected Sharon's mother to be at least a little like her own mother, and had been surprised to discover that Mrs. Eberhard was more like an old, but comfortable, shabby overstuffed sofa. She had arms thick as fence posts, an enormous stomach, graying mouse-colored hair, and clothes that looked as if they had been manufactured for her by an upholsterer. The Eberhards' Cape-Cod brick house was very much like Mrs. Eberhard. It was always filled with the lingering smells of cooking, usually something made with onions. Mrs. Eberhard spent half her life in the kitchen, Lizabeth decided. All the furniture in the house was well-worn, comfortable, and rarely free of piles of newspapers, year-old magazines, recipe clippings, toy trucks, school books, and unfolded laundry. The only room in the house that was neat, and except for tonight it was always extraordinarily neat, was Sharon's room.

Still, Lizabeth always enjoyed coming to the Eberhards' house. Though she was uncertain sometimes how she felt towards Sharon, she liked being around Mrs. Eberhard. The one thing she didn't like about being at the Eberhards' was the twins. They were terrible pests, and she didn't blame everyone for yelling at them.

Sharon finished painting Lizabeth's eyelids and stepped back to admire the reflection of her handiwork in the mirror.

"Well, I got on too much black," she said, quite unnecessarily. "But you know something, Lizabeth? You have beautiful eyes. They're really green and slanty. You look a lot like your mother now." Sharon sounded as if this were the supreme compliment.

Lizabeth wondered if she didn't look more like a panda bear with the black rings around her eyes, but she was too excited to worry about it. She was actually far more excited than she ever thought she'd be, giggling wildly along with the other Pop-Pop Girls as they bumped into one another trying to dress in Sharon's little room, trying to sit still while someone else fussed with her hair and face, watching the girls flit past the mirror like pastel butterflies in their flapper dresses and headbands drifting in plumes of lacy white feathers.

Lizabeth's mother had made the headbands for all of them, painting a different design on each with colors to match their dresses. "My friend Lizabeth's mother, the artist!" Sharon had said when Lizabeth pulled the

headbands from their box. She seemed far more impressed with the headbands than with all the work the mothers had done on the dresses. She said she was going to frame hers when the show was over.

As Sharon squeezed onto the dresser bench beside Lizabeth to build more makeup onto her own face, Lizabeth adjusted her headband over her forehead and turned to examine herself shyly in the mirror. She rather liked her green satin dress even if it was cut so low that her two skinny-bumpy collarbones stuck out. The satin was hot, but it felt smooth against her arms. She watched two glistening beads of perspiration roll out from under the spit curls in front of each ear, and wished she dared smile at herself in the mirror. But she wasn't going to do it. She had always thought it embarrassing to be caught smiling at yourself in a mirror.

Still, she was beginning to look not quite so much like a panda bear after all. Once you got used to them, the black rings really did make her eyes look greener, more slanty. But were her eyes beautiful? she wondered. She had never thought there was a single thing about her that was beautiful, and had often wondered how two such handsome people as her parents could have produced anyone as plain as she was. Now Sharon had said her eyes were green and slanty and beautiful. *Were* they?

Would *Loren* think so?

Suddenly, Lizabeth saw the corners of her mouth rise up in the faintest Cheshire-cat smile. She only hoped that Sharon hadn't noticed it. But Sharon was much too busy smiling at herself in the mirror to notice anyone else.

A half hour later, they were sitting at their desks in the classroom watching Mrs. Poole trying to get everyone's attention.

"Quiet! Quiet please!" Mrs. Poole rapped on her desk with a pencil. "Well, that's better. Now, let me see, I believe everyone is here—um—um—um." She hummed into a notebook, tapping down it with the pencil. "Gregory Leecey, are you here? Gregory, please raise your hand if you're here! Gregory—is—here." Mrs. Poole's pencil tapped Gregory Leecey into her notebook. "Well then, we're all here. Splendid!"

Dody shot her hand into the air and began waving it wildly. "Nobody in the stage crew is here yet, Mrs. Poole!"

Lizabeth knew where the three members of the stage crew were. But Loren was one of them, so she stared blankly ahead and waited for someone else to offer the information. She was pleased with herself for remembering to be so careful.

"Thank you, Dorothy," said Mrs. Poole with a polite little beam in her direction. "The stage crew isn't supposed to be here. They're already on stage. Now then"—she studied the clock over the blackboard—"I believe we can leave for the auditorium. So, let us proceed qui-et-ly down the hall in a neat line to the door on this side of the auditorium. Remember please, qui-et-ly!"

Sharon raced over to grab Lizabeth's hand, and then rushed her along with the other Pop-Pop Girls to stand in line behind the Washboard Band. Lizabeth thought the boys looked ridiculous in their electric-green-and-orange cardboard bowler hats and huge red crepe-paper bow ties, but she wasn't surprised to find that the rest of the girls thought they were adorable.

Everyone proceeded in a neat row out the door, but once they had left Mrs. Poole's watchful eye, they straggled the rest of the way down the hall to the auditorium. They had been told that they were to stay in the hall until their act was called for. But as soon as they arrived at the auditorium, the boys shoved themselves through the door to see the fifth-grade acts in progress. After a short, whispered conference to decide that their popcorn beads and dresses probably wouldn't get crushed, the girls followed the boys in. Two members of the stage crew hissed at them to get out, but since Mrs. Poole had stopped to talk with another teacher in the hall and there seemed to be no teachers in immediate evidence on that side of the stage, the Washboard Band moved in closer, followed by the girls. Other members of the class pushed in behind them.

Lizabeth saw Loren at once, perched on a tall stool by the curtain in his familiar gray sweatshirt, his hands around the curtain ropes. But though the others crowded around him to get a better view of the stage, paying no attention to him, Lizabeth stepped away from him into the shadows by the curtain wall. There she saw clearly everything that happened next.

Not content with standing quietly to watch someone else perform, Dennis Stickley began shifting his feet back and forth. His eyes darted restlessly around the back of the stage. Finally, from the look on his face, Lizabeth could tell that he had spotted something interesting. A moment later he was edging toward a large can of white paint. The paint had been used on the backdrop for the show, but now sat forgotten on the floor by the open curtain, directly behind Loren. Dennis picked up a brush resting against the can, flicked off the lid with the toe of his shoe, then dipped the brush into the paint. After wiping some of the paint on the edge of the can, he began jabbing the brush into the air as if he were dueling. Dody and Sharon saw him and giggled. Then Martha and Betsy turned to look. When Dennis saw that he had an audience, he started showing off even more, all the time jabbing the brush closer and closer to Loren. Then his hand darted out, and suddenly there was a broad stripe of white paint running down the back of Loren's sweatshirt. The four girls gave a gasp of horror and appreciation.

Loren turned quickly to look over his shoulder and saw both the paint on his sweatshirt and the wet brush in Dennis's hand. He let go of the curtain ropes and swung around. His jaw was tight, and even in the dimness of backstage, the knuckles of his clenched hands showed white against his jeans. But all he did was stare at Dennis. He never raised his hands or said a word. Dennis shrugged as if to say that it was an accident, but turned a fakey-innocent grin on the girls at the same time.

"Hey, curtain, curtain!" Tom hissed at Loren. "Jerk! You're supposed to close the curtain."

As the fifth-grade act trooped off the stage, the curtain moved haltingly across to close them off from the audience. "Jeez! He can't even pull a curtain," Tom broadcasted in a crystal-clear whisper.

In the shadow of the stage wall, Lizabeth pleaded

101

silently for Loren to do something to Dennis—*anything*. What was wrong with him that he didn't pick up the paintbrush and wipe the stupid grin from Dennis's face? Being sorry for him and furiously angry with him at the same time made her sick and weak inside. It was a strange and painful mixture of feelings she had never had before.

⁻ She had thought Loren was making it so easy for her, saying they could be secret friends. But where was she going to hide her feelings over something like this? She had never particularly liked the way everyone treated Loren at school when she still knew him as C.D., but then she hadn't really disliked it either. It came to her that she hadn't thought much about it at all. Now she *had* to think about it, and that was *not* easy.

Perhaps there was nothing easy about friendship with Loren, any kind of friendship, even a secret one. Perhaps that was why he had no friends. And perhaps she should never have written that note, and never go back to the house again.

"Come on, Lizabeth! What's wrong with you? We're on next!" Lizabeth felt Sharon grab her by the wrist. With the white stripe screaming at her from the back of Loren's shirt, she felt herself pulled from the shadows and toward the bright lights of the stage.

Mrs. Champlain, the school's musical director, began thumping out the opening bars of "By the Beautiful Sea," and Lizabeth somehow danced out onto the stage with the Pop-Pop Girls, a forced paper-doll smile on her face. She was grateful now for all the hours they had spent rehearsing. They had practiced the song and the dance and even the smiles so many times, she could perform like a mechanical doll, waving her arms and legs around, opening and closing her mouth as if she'd been wound up with a key. Even so, it was a long three-and-a-half minutes before they pranced off the stage.

Lizabeth would have been happy to wait in the hall until the show ended, as they were supposed to, but it was Dody's *geniusy* idea to sneak around to the back of the auditorium so they could watch the Washboard Band from there. Lizabeth had no choice but to sneak with them.

The Washboard Band was the last act, but it should have been the first, Lizabeth felt, to get it out of the way. Through the whole performance, Dennis Stickley stared at the audience with a vacant grin on his face as he plucked his washtub-and-broomstick bass fiddle. Bob Weiss continuously lowered his hands from his tissue-paper comb to scratch himself under his armpits, imitating a monkey. The others were doing equally silly things in a clear attempt to disguise their lack of talent by trying to be funny. Though they seemed to be enjoying each other hugely, the audience wasn't laughing much. Tom Leggett did make one effort to be serious in playing a short solo on his trumpet, but he was so terrible it was embarrassing. It was a relief when the band marched off the stage. No one applauded too much, not even the Pop-Pop Girls. The curtain floated smoothly across the stage, the auditorium lights came on, and they all ran to find their parents.

A few minutes later, the girls and their mothers and fathers were clustered together at the punch and cookie table. Sharon, Martha, Betsy, and Dody were giggling and repeating their Charleston steps to impress anyone who might be watching. The mothers and fathers were saying how charming the girls had been, and trying to find something else to say to one another. Lizabeth took tiny sips from her paper punch cup and let her eyes roam from one stage door to the other. When no one that interested her came through, she turned to the back of the auditorium. The white stripe on the gray sweatshirt was like a beacon in the far corner. Lizabeth felt her heart jump, but she went on calmly sipping her punch beside her father and mother, glancing up secretly over the rim of the cup.

Loren was standing with a very tiny red-haired woman neatly dressed in a trim dark blue dress and sweater. She didn't reach much above his chin. When Lizabeth and Loren had talked about their families in the house, he had told her that he'd lived with his grandmother ever since his parents were killed in a car crash when he was nine. This must be Loren's Mimi, Lizabeth decided. The two of them were standing alone.

Lizabeth felt happy when Mrs. Poole went over to speak to them for a few minutes. But Mrs. Poole soon drifted away from them to speak to another set of parents. Then Loren took his grandmother's arm and led her to the back door of the auditorium. Lizabeth found herself staring at the doorway even after it had swung shut and only the exit light was left to stare back at her.

She knew that she was no more going to stay away from the house and from Loren than she had before.

104

She would meet him there as they'd planned. She had never seriously considered anything else. Anyway, school would be over in a week. There would be no more confused feelings, no more hurt over what could happen there. It would truly all be easy then, simple and uncomplicated. Secret house, secret friend, secret summer—that was all.

Lizabeth set her punch cup down on the table. She wiped the whiskers of raspberry punch away from her mouth with the back of her hand, forgetting that Sharon had painted a huge Cupid's bow of lipstick on her. Then she reached for two Nabisco sugar wafers and turned to her mother and father. Her mother really did have green slanty eyes, she noticed, and her father looked particularly handsome in his navy wool blazer and white turtleneck shirt.

She wished it wasn't just Wednesday night. That made Saturday still two whole days away.

Chapter 9

THREE PEBBLES lay on the windowsill waiting for her when she arrived at the house Saturday afternoon. Lizabeth felt a strange little thump in her chest when she saw them. With a book that she had just brought from the library tucked firmly under one arm, she lifted the window and slid over the sill.

The splintered wood scraped her bare leg as it always did, leaving a pleasant, familiar tingle on her warm skin. But it gave her a strange feeling to see the room just as it was the very first time she peered through the window, empty except for the two rocking chairs that still faced each other silently, like two old men who had long since said all they could think of to say to one another. Dust had begun to settle thickly again on the floor. Lizabeth felt like a ghost, returning to haunt its old home. It was hard to believe that anyone real had ever been there, or that anyone was even there now. She stood for a moment, listening, and then heard the squeaking of the floorboards over her head. She started eagerly across the floor, but when she went through the glass doors, she stopped, feeling suddenly confused and shy.

Who was this boy she was running to meet upstairs? For a week they hadn't spoken to one another. Their eyes hadn't even met. She still had the picture in her mind of him sitting dumbly behind a stage curtain with a wide stripe of white paint down his back. Was this actually the same boy she had met here a week ago? Hesitantly, Lizabeth climbed the stairs.

He was leaning against a windowsill with his hands in his jeans pockets and his feet crossed loosely. He was looking toward the doorway. As soon as he saw her, his face opened up in a wide grin, and the strange thick feeling in her chest melted. This *was* the same boy! It was Loren of the secret house.

"Hi!"

"Hi!"

They stood for a moment, smiling at one another, and then Lizabeth looked across the room and cried out, "What's that?"

Directly opposite the fireplace, strewn from wall to wall, was the oddest assortment of things she had ever seen. In one corner, in front of the closet door, was a tattered lady's dress form on a stand. Beside it was a badly dented tarnished-brass birdcage with a great gap in it where wires were missing. A frayed carpet, which might once have been green, had been rolled up and tied with string, and now lay stretched across the room like a decaying tree trunk. Scattered around it were two small round oak tables with varnish yellowed and

107

cracked, at least three nondescript chipped vases, a disreputable-looking olive-green lampshade, a number of old picture frames, a drooping table lamp, an old, but still partly shiny chrome electric coffee maker, and a battered wooden table clock with its face missing. There were countless other things, too, but this was all Lizabeth could take in at the moment. She stood staring at it with round eyes.

Loren shook his head ruefully. "It's just stuff," he said. "Junk! Everything! You name it, it's probably there." He walked over to the unusual display on the floor, and with his hands on his hips, stood looking down on it, grimacing.

"But—but how did it all get here?" stammered Lizabeth.

"Through the window and up the stairs," Loren said in a teasing voice. Then he laughed. "*I* brought it. Who else?"

"I know *that,*" said Lizabeth seriously. Still puzzled, she studied the lady's form and the birdcage. "I mean, where did you find all these things?"

"Well, I happened to remember that Morris and Georgie go around on trash pick-up days before the garbage man comes, and they get all kinds of 'neat' stuff. At least, that's what Morris calls it. I decided to get up early on trash morning and beat them to it. Morris is right about one thing—there is lots of stuff. I'm not sure about the 'neat' part of it, though. You know something funny?" Loren shrugged. "I thought every one of these things was really spectacular when I was lugging it up the stairs. Now it looks like what it was supposed to be—garbage!"

Lizabeth began to laugh.

"What's funny?" Loren asked.

"You!" replied Lizabeth. "You remind me of me when I made my magic spell for the mantel. I thought it was beautiful until you looked at it. Then it looked stupid."

"But this really is stupid. I know you said you liked old things, but I'll bet you didn't mean anything like this. It's just junk!"

"No, it isn't, Loren!" said Lizabeth indignantly. "We can fix it up, clean the things and mend some of them, and use them all in the house. Everything looks so—so *interesting*."

Loren's eyes brightened hopefully. "You mean it?"

"Yes, I mean it!" said Lizabeth with a firm toss of her head. "Oh, I love fixing things up!" She clasped her hands together, sighing happily. As she did, the book she held under her arm slipped and thudded onto the floor. Loren darted for it.

"Hey, *The Lord of the Rings!*" As he turned the book in his hands, his face flushed with pleasure.

"I got it at the library," Lizabeth said. "It's the first one of the three, isn't it?"

"Yes, and you know I recognize it?" Loren grinned. "I think it's the same ratty copy I was reading before I got my own paperbacks."

"There was a brand-new one there in a plastic jacket," Lizabeth said quickly. "It had better print and everything. But I took this one. I don't know why."

"I do," said Loren. "Because it was so ancient." He smiled appreciatively at Lizabeth. "You really are a nut!"

"I told you I liked old things," said Lizabeth. "Anyway, I'll put it on this table for now. The table will be our library."

"We ought to bring our own books, though—ones we can keep—and not borrow them from the city," Loren said.

"Oh, we will!" With a sigh of satisfaction, Lizabeth gazed on the pile of old treasures that lay at her feet.

"Hey! Guess what?" Loren said suddenly. He lifted up a large brown grocery sack from behind the rug.

Loren, Lizabeth was discovering, had a remarkable ability to change the subject without warning. It was fun and interesting, but also confusing.

"I couldn't begin to," she said.

"I brought us a picnic! You aren't by any chance hungry, are you?" Loren looked at her hopefully.

"Starving!" said Lizabeth, and meant it. Having remembered just before lunch that she wanted to stop at the library for the book before going to the house, she had only had half an apple and a glass of milk before racing out the door.

Loren peered into the sack and looked up with a wry grin. "Well, it's sort of a lunch, anyway. Have a seat!" He waved a hand over the rug.

A small cloud of dust flew up as they dropped onto it, and Loren began an exaggerated fit of coughing and choking. Lizabeth rewarded his performance with a burst of appreciative giggles. When they had both settled down at last, Loren dipped into the sack. A few moments later, he had lined up on the floor in front of them two bottles of Coke, a thermos jug, a package

110

of Oreos, a box of Fig Newtons, and a package of pretzels.

"And last but not least," Loren said, "a bottle opener and a package of peanuts for Nutsy."

"Nutsy!" exclaimed Lizabeth.

"What's wrong?" Loren said, laughing. "Did you forget him?"

"Not exactly," said Lizabeth sheepishly. "Just this afternoon I forgot him."

"He forgives you," Loren said. "He was up here on the veranda roof just before you came. We can put some of these peanuts out there for him right now." He pulled a handful of peanuts from the package and gave the rest to Lizabeth.

They went to the window, and Loren unlatched and slid it up. Then, as they were leaning on the sill, laying the peanuts carefully on the shingled roof so they wouldn't roll off, Lizabeth remembered something that had puzzled her earlier.

"You know," she said, "I still wonder how the latch on the window downstairs got broken, the one we climb through. The other windows, like this one, you can only open from inside. Do you suppose someone broke in once, Loren, *really* broke in, like a hobo or an escaped criminal or something?"

Loren's hand stopped motionless in midair for a moment; then he shrugged and went right on steadily laying peanuts on the roof. "Who knows?" he said. "Anyway, it was lucky for us."

"Yes, it was," Lizabeth said, disappointed that Loren sounded so uninterested in the subject. She thought it mysterious and rather frightening, and

111

wanted to go on talking about it. "Well, I wonder—" she began.

"Hey!" Loren interrupted her. "I think I'll go out there and see if Nutsy has any acorns stored in the drainpipe."

"Loren!" Lizabeth cried, forgetting about the broken latch. "You wouldn't go out there!" The old green shingles looked slippery, steep, and dangerous. The roof seemed a place for squirrels, not people.

"I already have a couple of times," Loren said calmly. Then he gave Lizabeth a wicked grin. "How do you suppose I discovered Nutsy's secret warehouse? Hey, look who's coming! Boy, that guy can smell a peanut a mile away!"

The bushy silver-gray tip of a tail had poked up suddenly at one corner of the roof, quivering like a curious antenna. It rose up, bringing with it the nose, ears, and bright black eyes of the squirrel. In silence, they watched him hop across the roof, pick up a peanut, crack the shell, and in a perfectly unhurried, relaxed manner, crunch away at the nutmeat, as if he had no idea that anyone was watching him from the window. But immediately after he had eaten a second peanut, he flicked his tail, and in a few swift hops, had disappeared back over the side of the roof.

"Oh," Lizabeth wailed. "I wanted to see him hide some of the peanuts."

"Never happen," Loren said. "He knows we're here. He'll be back long after we're gone. Come on." He slid the window down. "Let's eat!"

When they had dropped once again onto the dusty rug, he said, "Hey, I almost forgot! Dessert—fresh and

112

unlaundered!" He pulled an unopened package of lemon Lifesavers from his jeans pocket and set it down in front of Lizabeth.

In her bed table drawer, Lizabeth happened to have three packages of lemon Lifesavers that she'd bought after Loren had given her the last one. But she didn't mention it, and only smiled and said, "I thought the soap gave them a very good flavor."

"You might have a point there," said Loren. "Now, how about something to drink? We have Cokes, and pink lemonade is in the thermos."

"Pink lemonade!" Lizabeth sighed wistfully. "I think that's what they must have had when they sat on the veranda at the summer house. Pink lemonade and little sandwiches—probably little watercress sandwiches." Lizabeth had never had a watercress sandwich in her life, but she loved the sound of it, like sprigged muslin.

"I'm sorry. I just didn't think about watercress sandwiches," Loren said, teasing again. "You wouldn't settle for a pretzel, would you?" He laughed and shook his head as Lizabeth dreamily held out her hand.

"I think I'll have the pink lemonade instead of the Coke, though, please," she said. "It's much more summer-housey."

Grinning at her, Loren suddenly lifted a cardboard box from behind the rug and handed it to her.

"What is it?" Lizabeth asked.

"Go ahead! Look inside." ·

Lizabeth lifted off the cover of the box, and she found that the box was filled with seashells.

"It's not exactly putting the house near the sea-

113

shore," Loren said apologetically. "But I thought it might help."

"Oh, Loren!" Lizabeth breathed. "It *does*. Houses by the seashore always have shells lying about everywhere." She jumped up and ran to the fireplace. "I'm going to put these on the mantel right now with the rest of the magic spell." She laughed over her shoulder at Loren. "Maybe we can conjure up an ocean!"

"We might try," Loren said suddenly. "Come along with me!" He started toward the doorway.

"Where are we going?" Lizabeth asked.

"No questions. Just come with me," said Loren mysteriously.

Lizabeth followed him down the stairs curiously. Then she followed him through the window, off the veranda, and finally down the slope that dropped away from the house. Lizabeth hadn't any idea how really wild it was back there, but creeping wild honeysuckle slithered across her bare legs, the stiff needles of stunted white pines jabbed out at her, and clouds of whining gnats rose up from nowhere and exploded against her skin. It seemed like a jungle.

"Is it much farther?" she asked in a small voice.

"I'm sorry," Loren said quickly. "I didn't stop to think how this would feel on your bare legs. Anyway, we're here, and there it is. I guess this doesn't make an ocean any more than shells make a seashore, but it's water."

In front of them a tiny stream curled its way along the sloping ground, finally losing itself in the twisted wild ivy and honeysuckle. Brown leaves and gray-green pebbles lay peacefully under the clear water.

"I'm glad you brought me. It's beautiful!" Lizabeth said. "You know, I thought I heard water the first day I came. Can you actually hear it from the house?"

"I don't know. After a hard rain, the spring that feeds this stream really bubbles up a storm." Loren laughed. "But I'm afraid maybe you just heard somebody watering his lawn."

"I don't care," said Lizabeth. "It's beautiful anyway."

"No sand for sand castles, though. I'll have to work on that."

"Hey!" said Lizabeth. "I'll bet you will."

Loren grinned. "Hey!" he said. "I'll bet I will too!"

Back in the house, they finished their cups of pink lemonade and all the Oreos, Fig Newtons, and pretzels they could hold, and then went to work sorting out and deciding where they should put everything. Loren had brought a hammer and nails and began driving nails in the walls for all the old picture frames—"Where they'll hang," said Lizabeth happily, "until we get the pictures." She already had visions of thumbing through piles of magazines to find just the right ones.

As the pounding of the nails thundered hollowly through the empty house, with echoes that seemed to crash right back into the room at them, Lizabeth perched on the rug, dreamily studying each battered treasure that Loren had brought. There seemed to be dozens of things she hadn't even seen when she'd first walked into the room. She picked up the old lampshade and found under it a tiny lavender-pink vase. Cupped in her hand, it looked and felt like a smooth, round plum. Strangely, it wasn't cracked or even chipped. As she sat admiring it, it came to her suddenly that several of the things she had looked at didn't seem at all like things someone would simply throw away in a heap of garbage. There was the set of brass candlesticks. Red wax had dripped down them from some long-ago candles, but they were not dented or bent. A set of carved-wood bookends were thick with a kind of sticky dust, but when Lizabeth had rubbed some of it off with a finger, she found that the finish under it was glossy, the carving whole and perhaps as nice as the day it was done.

"Loren?" said Lizabeth.

Loren turned to her, his hammer poised in mid-air. "What?"

"Did you find *all* these things just sitting in heaps waiting for the garbage man? I mean, some of them seem too nice for someone to want to throw away."

Loren went back to his nail and gave it a small tap. "What things?" he asked evenly.

"Well, how about this little vase? It's beautiful, and it's perfect. So are those candlesticks. And that lady's dress form. I know it's old and faded, but I just don't think anyone would throw it away in the garbage!"

Loren pulled a nail from his pocket and seemed to be concentrating very hard on holding it against the wall, as if it took a great deal of thought. "Some of the things came from our attic—Mimi's old stuff that she doesn't care about. I don't know why I forgot to mention that." He smiled over his shoulder at Lizabeth. "Okay?"

Lizabeth didn't know why he forgot to mention that either. It seemed strange, but she didn't know what she should say about it, especially with Loren smiling at her the way he was. "Okay," she said.

Loren went back to pounding nails.

"Was that Mimi with you at the school show Wednesday night?" Lizabeth asked.

Loren turned to her with a sudden grin. "Hey! I didn't know you'd seen us. We were way in the back of the auditorium."

"I'm sorry I didn't get to meet her," Lizabeth said. "I really would like to."

"No kidding? She'd like to meet you too. I've told her about you."

"When may I?" asked Lizabeth.

"Heck, any old time," said Loren.

"Now?"

"You mean, *right now?*"

Lizabeth nodded, but she was beginning to feel a little foolish because of the surprised look on Loren's face. Actually, she wasn't certain why she meant *right now,* except she thought it had something to do with Loren's forgetting to tell her everything about what he'd brought to the house. Suddenly, it had made her feel that she wanted to meet someone, almost anyone, who called him *Loren,* and not *C.D.*

But when he kept looking at her with a funny, shut-off look on his face, she said quickly, "We don't have to if it's not all right."

Loren started as if she'd just wakened him from a deep sleep. "Sure, sure, it's all right. It's great, in fact! Hey! Come on. Let's go."

He sounded so pleased about it now that Lizabeth wondered if she weren't just imagining a lot of things. Still, he was strangely quiet as they left the house and started up the path toward the street.

Chapter 10

"WELL, I guess we're here," Loren said. He sounded as if he were trying to swallow the words.

"But—but," Lizabeth stammered, "you never told me that you lived right next door!"

"You never asked me," said Loren, attempting a smile. "Does it make a difference?"

"I don't know," Lizabeth said. She thought it over a moment. "I guess not."

She smiled back at Loren, but then they walked the rest of the way to the large rose-brick house in silence. Lizabeth wasn't certain why, but it *did* make a difference, and suddenly she almost wanted to cry.

The minute they were inside the oak door, Loren said quickly, "Do you mind waiting here? I'll go get Mimi." He shot off as if someone had fired a starting pistol.

Lizabeth did mind. It felt lonely and odd being left to stand in an entry hall. She and Loren had suddenly become strangers, and she wished she'd never suggested coming.

But he had barely stepped into the adjoining dining room when the swinging door from the kitchen burst open and Loren's grandmother flew out. She was red-haired and tiny, just as Lizabeth remembered her, and she seemed to be lost in, rather than wearing, a huge striped apron that enveloped her like an Arabian tent.

"I've brought someone to see you, Mimi," Loren said. He didn't sound at all thrilled about it, but Mimi didn't seem to notice it.

"I see that you have!" She brushed past him into the hall, at the same time reaching behind her back to untie her apron. "Oh, what's the point of yanking it off? You've already seen me in it now. My dear, please forgive me! I don't usually run around draped in this glorified bath towel, but I was preparing to knead some dough, and that always calls for extensive covering."

"Oh, it's all right. My knees are dirty!" said Lizabeth, and then felt she must be turning a flaming red. It was an idiotic thing to say, and she couldn't imagine why she'd done it.

"Don't be embarrassed, my dear, either for saying it or having them!" Mimi smiled. It was a smile that made her look remarkably like Loren, Lizabeth noticed. "Dirty knees on someone your age are a sign that she's been having a good time. Now then, young man, why haven't you introduced us? Loren"—her tone of voice changed suddenly—"are you all right?"

"Sure, I'm all right," Loren said. "Mimi, this is

120

Lizabeth. Lizabeth, this is my grandmother, Mrs. Hunter. She likes to be called Mimi, though." He ended up this introduction with what almost passed for a smile.

Mimi looked at him for a moment as if she wasn't quite satisfied with what she saw; then she smiled again at Lizabeth. "Indeed I do! When someone addresses me as Mrs. Hunter, I often turn around to see if they aren't talking to the person behind me. Well then, so you are Lizabeth! How nice of you to let Loren bring you to meet me. You know, I saw you in your performance at the school last week. That was a charming act you were in. It was the high spot of the whole evening."

"I looked like a panda bear," said Lizabeth. "I mean, with all the black around my eyes."

"Nonsense!" Mimi laughed. "You looked no such thing. You probably don't know it, but you have to put on two or three times as much makeup as ordinary to have even the tiniest bit show on stage. I remember that specifically from my days in little theater. You looked delightful on stage in your green dress. Now then, why don't you and Loren come with me into the kitchen so that I can have some company while I finish my work, after which we'll consider refreshments."

"Are you building me a pizza, Mimi?" Loren asked.

"Yes, I'm building you a pizza. From the ground up!" she added to Lizabeth. "There was a day, you know, when all that was expected of a grandmother was apple pies and ginger cookies. Now we construct pizza pies!"

121

It seemed to be in spite of himself, but Loren finally grinned. "You could use a mix, Mimi."

"Mix, fiddlesticks! Now, let us proceed to the kitchen."

They passed through the dining room into a large room that seemed to Lizabeth to be four times as large as any kitchen she'd ever seen. Saucepans gleamed softly all around her on the walls like copper moons, and in the center of the floor was an enormous wooden table set out with crockery bowls, a well-worn sifter, packets of yeast, a tin saltshaker, and a sack of flour. A powdering of the flour already lay like fine snow on the floor around the table.

Lizabeth watched in fascination as Mimi went to work sifting, measuring, and stirring the ingredients in a bowl, then finally flopping all of it out onto the table.

"Is that going to be a pizza crust?" asked Lizabeth. All that had come out of the bowl was a crumbled white mound no bigger than a tennis ball. It looked like one of her own cooking failures.

"That is my fond hope!" Mimi said. "But first, of course, it has to be kneaded, then allowed to rise, and then stretched and stretched like a balloon. If I don't goof, as Loren puts it, it should end up a pizza crust."

"Would you like some help?" Loren asked.

"As long as you're here, that would be splendid," Mimi said. She looked at him sharply. "Are you quite certain you're all right, Loren?"

"Heck yes, Mimi, I said I was okay!"

Mimi raised her eyebrows at him. "Well, if you say so. You don't have to scowl at me like that. I'm sorry if I'm embarrassing you. You know, pizza dough is exactly like India rubber." Mimi sailed right back to her conversation with Lizabeth as if there hadn't been any interruption at all. "To work it takes muscle. I appreciate all the help I can get, when it's available. Uh-uh-uh!" she said as Loren raised his hands over the dough and was about to descend on it. "First a trip to the sink, young man, where you will run your hands over the soap and under the faucet—twice!"

As Loren shrugged and retreated to the sink, Lizabeth examined her own hands and found they were coated in dirt, dust, and the sticky remnants of pink lemonade and Fig Newtons. "I think I ought to wash mine too," she said. "May I borrow the sink, Mrs.— I mean, Mimi?"

"Of course you may borrow the sink," said Mimi. "Provided you return it." Lizabeth liked not having Mimi smile when she said this.

As she let cool water dribble over her hands at the sink, Lizabeth wondered at how at home she felt, how really comfortable and contented, like a puppy in a basket by the furnace. Now she was terribly glad that she'd come. Mimi had made all the strange things she'd been imagining melt away as if they were Jell-O in the hot sun. It reassured her, too, to know that Mimi didn't think Loren was acting himself. Lizabeth wondered if she should say anything about Loren's shoveling down a column of Fig Newtons, half a package of Oreos, a

123

cup of pink lemonade, and both their Cokes. Loren had assured her that he had a cast-iron stomach, but maybe he didn't.

Lizabeth began to hum. She looked around at the little china measuring cups and spoons dangling from hooks at the side of the cabinet, the blue-and-white Dutch tiles behind the faucet, and the flat Japanese bowl with a miniature pine tree growing in it. Beside it was a round, fat little lavender-pink vase.

"Loren!" Lizabeth twisted her head around excitedly. "This little vase—it's exactly like the one—oh!" She threw a dripping hand to her mouth.

"Why, yes," said Mimi calmly. "I wondered if you'd recognize it. It's a twin to the one Loren brought to the house. I gave it to him to give to you as I had a feeling from what he'd told me that—" Mimi stopped suddenly. She looked from Lizabeth to Loren, and back to Lizabeth again. "So that's it! I can see from your faces. Loren, dear child, you haven't told her yet, have you?"

Loren's face had gone almost as white as the lump of dough he was now studying carefully, as if he were trying to read some kind of message in it.

"A lie built on a lie built on a lie. It never works. My dear," Mimi said to Lizabeth, "while I stay out here and finish up my work, why don't you dry your hands, stop looking so worried, and run along with Loren to the den. I believe he has something he wants to tell you."

They sat across from one another with the fireplace between them, and stared at their shoelaces, just as they once had done at the secret house. It was like going back to the beginning of the game, Lizabeth thought suddenly.

Loren didn't start out with any complicated excuses. He just said, "The house belongs to Mimi, Lizabeth, so I guess you'd say it belongs to me too. Mimi bought it a year ago. I told you it was my secret house because it sounded like a good idea when I heard it from you. Before you came around, I just walked through the front door with a key. The way the window latch got busted was when I was trying to open it one day to give Nutsy a cracker and shoved on it when it wasn't properly unlatched. I pulled those crossed boards off the front windows, too, in case you wondered."

Lizabeth couldn't think of a word to say except to herself. Her secret house wasn't a secret after all! Loren must really have been laughing at her. All that climbing in the window, pretending this and pretending that—what a huge joke it must have been for him What a *creepy* trick to play on her! Tears stung Lizabeth's eyes as she finally tore them away from staring at her shoelaces.

"Don't look at me like that! Please don't!" Loren said.

"Why didn't you tell me?"

"Mimi told me to, but I didn't dare. Look, do you remember that first day you found me in the house, and you started to leave because you said I'd come there first so that made it *my* house. Well, once you *did* leave, I knew you'd start thinking it over. Heck, you'd started thinking it over even before you left. Here was old Creepy Douglas, and there you were, Lizabeth Bracken, member of the V.I.B.'s and G.'s, sharp new girl in the sixth grade. Would you have ever come back if you'd known that it was *really* my house?"

Lizabeth hesitated. "I don't know," she said honestly.

"Well, I do, because to tell you the truth, if I'd been in your place, I wouldn't have. Anyway, thanks for not lying about it."

There was a silence as they both returned to their shoelaces. Then Lizabeth found that she was smiling as a thought came to her. "I didn't know I was the sharp new girl in the sixth grade."

"Are you kidding!" Loren exploded. "You're sharp and smart, and you're nice too. Why do you think Sharon Eberhard latched onto you five minutes after you came to Anderson Bays? You're not even stuck on yourself like the rest of those girls. When I got up out of that rocking chair and discovered it was you that had wandered in through the window, I nearly passed out. I wasn't going to push my luck, telling you all about the house. I figured that even if it wasn't me you'd discovered there, you might not come back because you'd think you were trespassing or something. You were pretty anxious about letting me know there wasn't any sign around. Hey! I hope you're not really mad at me."

"I guess I was for a minute," Lizabeth said, "thinking about how you were laughing at me all along."

126

"Laughing at you!" Loren slapped his forehead. "You must be off your nut! I was so scared the whole time that I'd let something slip, I was quivering in my sneakers. I couldn't believe, when you started asking questions this afternoon, that I'd been such a big jerk as to let Mimi talk me into taking all that stuff from our house. She didn't know that I hadn't clued you in yet to the house. I was really scared to bring you over here today without telling her first. You may have noticed."

"I noticed!" said Lizabeth. "Has Mimi known about me from the beginning?"

"From the beginning," Loren said. He threw out his hands in a gesture of despair. "Oh, well!"

All at once laughter choked up inside Lizabeth, and she couldn't hold it back.

"What's funny?" Loren said.

"Everything!" gurgled Lizabeth. "It's all funny!"

"Hey! You know something? It really is—I *think*."

"It *is*," said Lizabeth. "*Me* climbing through the window like a heroine in a mystery story!"

"*Me* making out like a storybook hero! Heck, if you'd been brave enough to climb into a deserted house through a window, I wasn't about to let you think my grandmother had let me through the front door with a key!" Loren grinned.

"We read too many books," said Lizabeth.

"No, it's not that we read too many. It's that we believe what we read!"

They looked at one another with a happy acceptance of the humor of the whole situation, and then

127

burst out laughing. They went on giggling and laughing and couldn't seem to stop.

"What on earth is all this merriment?" Mimi said, appearing suddenly in the doorway. "Am I to assume that everything has been straightened out to everyone's satisfaction?"

Lizabeth looked at Loren. They nodded at one another. Then Lizabeth giggled behind her hands, and they both fell back into their chairs, laughing.

"Splendid!" said Mimi. "I felt it would be." She peeled off her baggy apron and seemed magically to shrink down to her correct tiny size in a Kelly-green pants suit. When she saw that Lizabeth had stopped gasping for air enough to carry on a conversation, she said, "My dear, I hope you've forgiven Loren for his deception."

Lizabeth looked at Loren again and nodded. "I'm sorry I was trespassing," she said quickly. "I didn't see a sign."

"There wasn't one. Those two little ruffians, Morris and Georgie, continually help themselves to ones I have put up, which merely say 'House Not For Sale.' But if you think I'm angry with you, child, I'm not a bit. I only admit to being nervous as a cat when Loren told me he'd found you in the house, worrying if anything should happen to you there. Do your parents know about the house? No, of course they *don't*. I can see by your look that they don't. Well, that's to be expected! Parents are not often clued in, as Loren would say, to such things as secret houses."

Mimi lowered herself into the chair next to Liza-

beth and looked down for a moment with a small, pleased smile on her face. "You know, when I was a young girl and lived in the country, my friend Delia and I had our own version of your secret house. But ours happened to be a very old, very shaky, and very dangerous barn, scheduled by the Almighty, we were warned in deep, foreboding tones, to go down at any moment in a windstorm. We really did enjoy that barn, swinging from the rotten rafters, looking for buried treasure, spinning our secrets like little spiders in the dark, pungent corners. It reeked of manure, of course, though animals were long since gone from it. I'm not certain how we stood it on hot, humid days. At any rate, our families were quite correct. The Almighty did have it in mind to dispose of the barn, although not by wind. He chose to hurl a bolt of lightning at it one night, and it quickly burned to the ground. Neither Delia nor I ever did tell our parents we'd been playing in the barn." Mimi looked tremendously self-satisfied with this announcement. "We never did tell them, even after we'd grown up!"

"Mimi, you never told me about that!" Loren said.

"Of course I didn't," Mimi said primly. "Anyway, I couldn't risk giving you any additional ideas to the ones you already have. This young gentleman is a terrible daredevil, Lizabeth—two broken arms, at one time or another, a concussion, and of course you can still see the evidence of one adventure, a chipped tooth! All of these events took place, fortunately, when he was not yet in my care, so I was spared having to suffer

130

through them. Nevertheless, though I've restrained my-
self from asking, undoubtedly from fear of knowing the
answer, I believe he still does such foolish and dangerous things as crawling out on that veranda roof!"

Loren seemed to be having some trouble trying to
give Mimi a blank, innocent look.

"Hey! Listen to that wind," Loren said. "I think
we're in for one."

As Mimi was talking, the room had grown darker
and darker, and a tall juniper began to scratch wildly
against the den windows as the wind gusted around the
corners of the house.

"I believe you're right," Mimi said. "We'd better
go around and check all the windows. Mercy, child!"
She bobbed her head at Lizabeth. "It's getting chilly,
and there you are in that thin little blouse and shorts.
You should have a sweater! Mine are all too small, I
believe, but Loren might have something to fit you.
Loren, when you've finished with the windows upstairs,
bring down your red sweater, the one your Aunt Mary
sent you. That will do nicely, I think."

Loren shrugged at Lizabeth to let her know that
there was no use in arguing with Mimi. A few minutes
later, Lizabeth was swimming in an enormous sweater
that she was certain must have been too big even for
Loren. It came down to the hem of her shorts.

"It makes me feel naked-legged," said Lizabeth.

Loren grimaced. "You'd better not mention it to
Mimi. She'll have you wrapped in a tea cozy if you're
not careful!"

131

"What's that about a tea cozy?" said Mimi. She came into the den with two glasses of milk and a plate of cookies on a tray.

"Nothing," said Loren, glancing at Lizabeth.

"I'm certain that neither one of you expects me to believe that," said Mimi tartly. "At any rate, Lizabeth, here are the home-baked cookies I tried to get Loren to take to the house this afternoon, but he kept insisting in his stubborn manner that it was *his* party." She served the cookies to Lizabeth and to a grinning Loren, who picked up six with one hand. Mimi didn't flutter an eyelash over it.

"You know, my dear," she said to Lizabeth, "it occurs to me that you might like to know how I came to own your secret house. Would you?"

"Oh, yes!" said Lizabeth. She didn't even wait to swallow her mouthful of oatmeal cookie.

"To tell the truth," Mimi said, "it happened so suddenly, it still rather surprises me when I remember that I now actually own it. The house had always been rented out by its owners until some ten years ago when they finally decided to sell it. The house even then was shabby and in need of many repairs, perhaps ready to be torn down, but Loren's grandfather and I had always thought we would love to have that marvelous piece of forested land right next to our own house. Unfortunately, a flinty, ill-tempered old gentleman named Mr. McPherson, who lived down the street, learned of the prospective sale before we did, and purchased the property from under our noses. As an investment, he said! Hmmmph!" snorted Mimi. "If you

132

want my opinion, he bought it for sheer meanness. He had more money than he knew what to do with, and no one to leave it to except two distant cousins he had never even met.

"We happened to have the same lawyer as Mr. McPherson, and for a number of years, we tried to persuade him, via Mr. Sumner, to sell us the property, but he absolutely refused. The stubborn old goat! He didn't rent the house or take care of it. It simply sat there. Finally, when Loren's grandfather died, I ceased thinking about the piece of land and the house altogether.

"A year ago, Mr. McPherson died, and Mr. Sumner called me to say that, as the cousins had no interest in the property, it would be sold. Was I still interested? he wanted to know. Well, the call caught me completely off guard. Still, I suppose I would have had the good sense to say 'no,' if this young gentleman sitting across from you, my dear, didn't talk me into it. In one moment of weakness, I agreed to buy it, and signed the contract on his birthday, which happened to be just three weeks short of a year ago!"

Lizabeth was so wrapped up in hearing the story that she didn't even recognize that the end of it had come. She kept on staring at Mimi.

"Good heavens! Did my story put you to sleep?" said Mimi, laughing.

"Oh, no!" Lizabeth said. "I was waiting for you to say what would happen to the house now."

"Do you know that I have simply no idea at all? Besides the original mischief of making me purchase the property, Loren has also persuaded me to do not one thing about the house or the land, for the time being at least, so that he can have it as a retreat." Mimi looked as if she were suppressing a smile. "From me, I suppose! Why, child," she exclaimed suddenly, "look at your legs. They're a mass of goose bumps! I'm going to look for the afghan. I wonder where I could have put it?"

Loren looked at Lizabeth. Lizabeth looked at Loren.

"Now, just what are you two grinning about?" said Mimi.

Chapter 11

LIZABETH BOUGHT HERSELF a little red diary with a lock on it. It was a five-year diary so there wasn't much room to write a lot for any day. On June fifth, for example, all she could get in was, *Today Loren and I unrolled the green rug. Lots of dust and dead moths.*

They had to sweep the rug because there was no electricity for plugging in a vacuum cleaner.

"My lungs will be ruined forever," Loren said. "You know, I'm giving up my life for it, and it still looks exactly like it came from the place where I found it—a garbage pile!"

"Would it help to sweep it some more?" asked Lizabeth.

"All we can do for that rug is pray for it," Loren said.

"Maybe we should go back to the attic and see if Mimi has a better one hiding someplace," Lizabeth offered brightly.

"I already have, and she doesn't, and it's raining."

"Oh," said Lizabeth.

Her diary continued:

June eighth: Sharon over to swim.

June twelfth: Loren and I hung Spanish shawl, travel posters, and pictures from Mimi's attic.

The picture they considered their choicest subject was one of a lanky lady, scantily dressed in gauze, sitting on a rock and gazing at blue bubbles seemingly released from a cloud over her head.

"Totally unsuitable!" Mimi said indignantly. "Why—why, I don't even know where it came from."

"I'll bet you don't!" said Loren. "Anyway, who cares? It's real jazzy."

"Whatever that's supposed to mean," said Mimi.

"It means that we want to take it. Heck, Mimi, she's dressed!"

"Well, I suppose she is. If you can call it that!"

They hung the picture in the select center spot on the wall.

June thirteenth: Sharon over to swim.

June sixteenth: Loren and I brought pillows from trunk in attic. Dressed Arabella.

They brought over armloads of pillows from the attic and banked them on either side of the fireplace. Some were plain old bed pillows in blue-and-white ticking, some were elaborate velvet and sateen pillows that were remnants of Mimi's "exotic" period, she told them, and a large number had such faded legends on

136

them as "Souvenir of Lake Onawanakakee," or names that sounded like that to Lizabeth.

Surveying all this elegance from across the room was Arabella, the dress form. Lizabeth had discovered that she was right about someone not putting it out for the garbage man.

"She's absolutely useless now," Mimi said, "but I wouldn't part with Arabella for anything. And wipe the grin off your face, young man," she said to Loren. "Give her to the city dump, hmmmph!"

Loren made a head for Arabella from an old cotton-stuffed hatstand, and Lizabeth painted a wide-eyed staring face on it. Then she dressed the form in a flowing lavender chiffon dress of Mimi's, resurrected from an old attic trunk, and crowned the head in a wide-brimmed straw hat floating in a sea of pale yellow ostrich feathers.

"Well, I have to admit it gives the room class," Loren said, after refusing to comment on it all afternoon.

"I think she's *elegant*," said Lizabeth.

June seventeenth: My first baby-sitting job—for Donny Dawes on the second floor. Yippee!

June twentieth: Sharon over to swim. No luck about her B. P.

Sharon's and Loren's birthdays turned out to be on the same day. Sharon expected Lizabeth to spend all afternoon helping her get ready for her party. Inventing a reason not to do it was too big a lie to tell. Besides, whatever kind of friendship theirs was, it was

137

still a friendship. You didn't pull stunts like that on friends.

"Oh, Lizabeth!" Sharon said. "I'm really glad you're going to help me with my party."

"So am I," Lizabeth said dimly.

June twenty-first: Discovered windup portable record player in attic. Seashells, pink lemonade, loud scratchy records—SUMMER HOUSE!

Loren and Lizabeth
Lizabeth and Loren
Loren and Lizabeth

The last had been squeezed into the diary in tiny letters no larger than grains of rice.

Chapter 12

MR. EBERHARD had promised to turn their basement into a proper recreation room with tiles on the floor, wood paneling on the walls, and maybe even a bar with little beer-can lights over it, Sharon told Lizabeth. But he could never find the time between his day job and his night job to do anything about it. Lizabeth wasn't surprised. Mr. Eberhard always seemed too tired to her to do anything at home except collapse in a chair. He was even too tired to talk, and was the most silent person she had ever known. When she first met him, he had held up his stump of a left forefinger and said with a funny little grin that another inch into the buzz, and he'd have been a nine-fingered carpenter. She heard him repeat this to her father at the school when she introduced them. That was about all he had to say. Talking seemed to be too much for him. Anyway, this year for Sharon's birthday, as with all the others, he still hadn't done anything about the basement.

Some attempt had been made to turn it into a recreation room. They had added a sagging sofa covered in red plastic, three bulging armchairs with stuffing bursting like grimy, gray popcorn through holes the twins had dug into the upholstery, a badly warped Ping-Pong table, and an old record player. But the room still looked like exactly what it was—a dark, dingy basement, smelling of sawdust, mildew, and Mrs. Eberhard's laundry soap.

Sharon and Lizabeth spent all afternoon trying to make it into something else.

"Are you sure it looks all right, Lizabeth?" Sharon asked. They were standing in the middle of the basement waiting for the first ring of the doorbell. It was about the tenth time since four o'clock in the afternoon that Sharon had asked Lizabeth the same question.

"It looks a lot better since we covered all the lights with blue paper," said Lizabeth. She was surprised at how much you could accomplish by turning down the lights to practically out.

"Do you think we have enough crepe paper and balloons?"

"We used up all we had, Sharon."

"Do you think we should have got some more?"

"No," Lizabeth said. "I think the lights are enough."

"Are you sure?"

"I'm sure. I really am. It looks nice, Sharon."

"Are you sure?"

"I'm sure," said Lizabeth.

She whirled around because she liked the feel of her long red calico skirt flying out and then swirling down around her bare legs. She was really feeling happy that night. She'd had fun helping Sharon that afternoon, and Sharon seemed ridiculously pleased to have her, as if the whole success of the party hung on Lizabeth's being there. And she went into raptures over the present Lizabeth brought. It was a pastel drawing her mother had done of the two of them by the swimming pool one afternoon. Mrs. Bracken had had it framed at the gallery for Lizabeth to give Sharon. Sharon had immediately hung it right by her bed.

Everything else had turned out right, too. She loved her new dress. "All that makeup" Sharon had insisted they wear for her party turned out to be nothing more than a little eye pencil and pink lipstick. And tomorrow Lizabeth was going to have a belated birthday party for Loren at the secret house. She was going to take cupcakes, made by herself, pink lemonade, and a very special present she had already bought. And she was going to wear this same new dress.

Lizabeth threw out her arms and whirled and whirled and whirled. Her dress flew out like a huge red parachute around her, as if she had jumped from a cloud and were floating across the whole world in it.

Within five minutes of the time the doorbell first rang, all twelve of Sharon's guests had either tripped daintily, if they were girls, or stampeded like cattle, if they were boys, down the basement steps.

141

Dody and Betsy put their blessing on Sharon's and Lizabeth's efforts. "Ooooooh! It's bea-u-tiful!" they squealed in a duet.

Sharon waited until everyone arrived before she perched on the arm of a chair and began tearing off the wrappings of her birthday gifts. They were all records, but Sharon oohed and aahed over each one, even the duplicates. Some of the girls had written poems.

"Whether this record be cool or hot,

When you play it, forget me not!" Sharon read aloud.

"Ugh! Ick! Blecch!" someone said approvingly.

There were a few other wise remarks made while Sharon pulled out the next one, which happened to be Dody's.

"Boys call us lemons, but boys are a tease,

'Cause aren't we the lemons the boys like to squeeze?"

"Hey! Hey! Hey!" said a boy's voice.

"Stolen right out of her autograph book!"

"What's that got to do with records, Dody?"

Dody smiled around archly at everyone, and kept her mouth shut.

Through all of this, Lizabeth stood around feeling shy and not quite knowing what to do with her hands and feet. As soon as Sharon had piled all her new records onto the player, and music began crashing through the basement, Lizabeth started gathering ribbons and torn wrappings from the floor so she wouldn't just be standing around. But as she was stuffing it all into a wastebasket, she felt a big nudge in her ribs.

142

Bob Weiss was standing in front of her whirling a finger in the air to indicate that he wanted a dance. By the end of two fast dances, Lizabeth had forgotten all about being shy. She played Ping-Pong on the warped table, squeezed into the sagging chairs with two or three other warm bodies, munching potato chips and Fritos and drinking Cokes, and then dancing again. She was having a very good time.

Within an hour, everyone was dripping wet, and the room was beginning to smell like gym. A couple of people pretended to gag and choke, but nobody really seemed to mind it.

"Hey, Sharon!" Dennis Stickley leaned over the back of a chair and poked her. "Great party!"

Sharon beamed as if she had just been awarded the Nobel Prize.

The change in the party started so gradually that at first Lizabeth didn't even know anything was happening. It was just Tom Leggett and Dennis Stickley hovering over the record player with their heads together, which wasn't anything unusual. Then Hank McGinnis joined them.

Lizabeth thought they were just picking out records to play, but then she noticed first one boy, and then another, stomp over to them and have a knee-slapping good laugh. She decided finally that they must be telling dirty stories. She knew from school that that was the way they usually acted when something along those lines was going on. Then they started calling over the girls.

143

The girls didn't slap their knees or carry on like lunatics, but they did smile and seem to approve of what they were hearing. Lizabeth wondered what she would do if she were called over to the record player. What if she didn't *get* the story? Or didn't think it was funny? Would she be able to smile or laugh as if she did, like the other girls? Thinking about it brought on a sudden leaden feeling in her stomach. She wished she hadn't drunk that last Coke.

But just as it seemed to be about her turn, Sharon appeared back in the basement with a fresh package of Fritos, and the boys hailed her over. Lizabeth watched her nod her head agreeably and then run back up the stairs. A few moments later, she reappeared breathlessly with a grocery sack, which she handed to Tom.

Tom flicked off the record player and waved the sack over his head with a triumphant grin. "Okay, everybody, we've got what we need now!"

"Watch out, stupid!" Dennis said. "You'll bust 'em."

"No way," Tom said. "Look, if everyone's ready, let's go!"

Lizabeth pushed her way over to Sharon and pulled her aside. "What's happening? I didn't know we were going anyplace," she whispered.

Sharon sighed impatiently. "They told me they'd told everyone about it. We're going to egg C.D.'s house."

Lizabeth felt as if her stomach were dropping right out of her. For a moment, she stared stupidly at Sharon. "What does that mean, to egg a house?"

"Oh, you know, Lizabeth!" Sharon was beginning to sound more irritated. "It's just where you throw eggs at someone's house."

"But why?" Lizabeth asked. She was surprised that it didn't come out a scream.

"No reason. It's just something to do." Sharon's eyes wandered restlessly to where everyone was gathering at the foot of the stairs.

"Aren't they all having a good time here?" Lizabeth persisted. "I thought everyone was having a good time."

"Sure, they're having a good time," Sharon said. She started to pull away from Lizabeth. "I *said* it's just something to do. We'll only be gone a few minutes. The boys all want to."

"Do you want to, Sharon?" Lizabeth asked.

Sharon turned on her sharply. "I have to go. It's my party, isn't it?" She paused, and then repeated, "I *have* to go."

"Well"—Lizabeth swallowed the sticky lump in her throat—"I don't want to go. I'll stay here and—and clean up or something."

"You can't do that, Lizabeth. What's wrong with you? They'll think it's funny if you don't go. We *all* have to."

"Hey, you two guys!" Tom shouted at them. "Let's get the show on the road. What's keeping you? Come on, Sharon!"

"C.D. is *waiting*," Dennis sang in his famous falsetto voice.

"We *all* have to go," Sharon repeated. She stared

coolly at Lizabeth, and then added in a stiff little voice, "Whether we want to or not."

Lizabeth discovered that a nightmare wasn't just something that happened to you when you were asleep. She was wide-awake and *in* one as she moved her legs mechanically down the streets, surrounded by squealing, giggling strangers, who somehow, somewhere she remembered as being her girl friends, and their hooting, howling monkey companions who, oddly enough, addressed each other as *man*.

"Okay, guys, we're only two blocks from C.D.'s house. Now shut up, everyone!"

At this command from their gallant leader, they all fell silent as they approached their target. In a few moments, they were lined up in front of the house.

It was dark across the front, but a light shone from a side room at the back. It was the kitchen, Lizabeth knew. Loren was probably in there now with Mimi, helping himself to his fourth or fifth slice of birthday cake. It would be a white cake with chocolate frosting. That was what he particularly liked, white cake with chocolate frosting.

They passed the paper sack around. Two girls giggled nervously, but otherwise there was silence as each one drew out an egg. They discovered that they were three eggs short. Lizabeth, huddled against a forsythia bush almost at the corner of the garden, didn't have to take one. The eggs ran out before the sack reached her. She didn't know who the others were who didn't get an egg. Then those who did have them began hurl-

ing them at the house, one by one. Splat! Splat! Splat! They burst against the steps and the door. They struck Mimi Hunter's camellias and her Charlotte Armstrong roses. One egg cracked against what might have been a metal faucet, and one of the boys gave a low whistle of approval.

Lizabeth didn't watch the eggs fly out or hit. But she could hear and feel every one of them as if they were hitting her. She felt the shells strike her arm or her face, burst open, and let the warm, sticky egg flow down her skin. Splat! Splat! Splat!

Lizabeth didn't understand how anything like this could be happening. When school ended, all of the confused feelings and the hurting were to have ended, too. Yet this was worse than anything that had happened at school, worse even than that night on the stage. She was just watching then. Now she was as much a part of what was happening as if she were hurling the eggs herself. And all she could do was cry out silently, "Loren!"

Loren! Loren! Loren!

It was just as Sharon had said—they were gone only a few minutes. In less than half an hour, they were back in the basement. Except for several attempts at getting laughs by trying to imitate with rude noises the sounds the eggs made hitting the house, nobody said much more about it. The party picked right up where it had left off. They danced, played Ping-Pong, and ate hamburgers with onion, mustard, and relish as if nothing had happened at all.

148

Chapter 13

LIZABETH WOKE THE NEXT MORNING so tired it seemed she hadn't slept at all. Her eyelids felt as if they had been rubbed with sand. She felt oddly heavy, as if she had gained a thousand pounds overnight. She had the strange feeling she couldn't move if she tried. The sun was squeezing spaghetti strings of light through the cracks in her blinds, and she listlessly counted fifteen of them lying across her legs. She wondered if they might not be tying her down.

She was glad she didn't have to get up right away. This wasn't one of the two mornings in the week when she baby-sat, and she could always miss the park program she'd finally signed up for. It was Book Talk Day, and she hoped in a weary kind of way that she wasn't missing a good one.

In the kitchen, miles away it seemed, the telephone rang. Calls in the morning were usually a wrong number or somebody trying to sell something. Lizabeth lifted a hand off the bed and was mildly surprised that she could move it. She felt that she ought to be getting up. There would be a note on the dining table from her mother saying something like, "Hi, sweetie! So happy you had such a good time at Sharon's party last night. You looked a little peaked, though, when Mr. Eberhard brought you home. Hope you had a good rest! Please call me at the gallery just as soon as you get up to let me know you're all right. Daddy flying in at six, so I'll go right to the airport from work. Love, Mother." This would be followed by a long row of kisses.

The telephone rang and rang and finally stopped. Could that have been her mother calling *her?* she wondered. She should go call her mother and find out. She should get up anyway. Someone had slopped hamburger relish down the front of her dress, and she had to wash that out, and then make the cupcakes for Loren's party.

Cupcakes for Loren's party! How unreal it sounded. What was real was eggs splattered across the front of a house. By now Loren would have seen them as he started out for his lawn-mowing jobs, and he couldn't help guessing how it had happened. What kind of party would they have that afternoon?

With a tired sigh, Lizabeth threw her right leg out from under the sheet. Now her bare foot stuck up over the sheet as if it didn't belong to anybody. She stared at it for a long time, sticking up so funny and bare such a long way from her chin. Then she finally dropped it to the floor. Some way, sometime, her day had to begin.

Nutsy sat on the veranda railing with his bright bead-black eyes fastened curiously on Lizabeth as she lay three pebbles on the windowsill, and then went to the front door and unlocked it with a shiny new key. It was as if he were wondering what she was doing walking through a front door now, instead of climbing in a window. Another time Lizabeth would have thought it funny.

Her large grocery sack brushing against her skirt, Lizabeth hurried across the living room, through the glass doors, and up the stairs. In the room, she kneeled before the fireplace and began quickly to empty the contents of the sack. First she unfolded four paper napkins and formed them into a large square on the floor. On them she formed a ring of twelve chocolate-frosted white cupcakes, and then set a peppermint-striped birthday candle in each one. On opposite sides of the ring, she placed a paper cup and napkin, and next to one cup, a book-shaped package in birthday wrapping. The last thing she did was blow up the four balloons she had brought, and set them on the hearth, where they lay quivering like giant soap bubbles. Then she sat back to review her work.

"Happy birthday!" read the bright red-and-yellow messages on the cups and napkins. How happy could this birthday be? Lizabeth wondered.

But what if—what if there were no birthday party

at all? What if Loren had finally given up on Lizabeth and her wonderful V.I.G.'s and B.'s? Wasn't that really the thought that was making her feel so dull and heavy, as if she had little weights tied to her arms and her legs and her brain?

The minutes dragged by as Lizabeth sat woodenly before the fireplace, shuffling a cupcake in or out to make a more perfect circle, as if it made any difference, straightening a candle that had fallen over in the rapidly softening chocolate frosting. The room was becoming unbearably hot, with the sun beating in through the side window. Lizabeth half thought she might throw open all the windows, never mind Morris and Georgie or secrecy or anything. But she didn't. She went on sitting. Under the waistband of her new red calico dress, she could feel the perspiration rolling down her skin in beads.

A half hour went by, and Loren had not come.

Lizabeth's legs began to cramp, so she stood up finally and began to wander aimlessly around the room. It seemed strange to her to have things that had seemed so alive when they were shared with someone, seem so lifeless now. There was Arabella in her ridiculous finery, staring across the room with wide eyes and caterpillar eyelashes that made her look as if she were in a continuing state of shocked surprise. How funny Arabella had seemed only two days before. Now, she was only a dress dummy.

The lady in the flimsy dress, perched on her mountaintop mysteriously gazing into the blue bubbles that

152

fell endlessly around her head, had become only a lady in a very bad picture. And the faceless clock that sat amidst all their other treasures on the shelf that was now their library—that was the thing Loren joked most about. "No time like the present." "My time is your time." "No time to spare." They were terrible jokes, and both of them knew it, but at the time it all seemed hysterically funny. Now, seeing the clock, Lizabeth felt a small dull ache. She looked at her watch and saw that fifteen more minutes had passed.

When she came to the old Gramophone on the floor by the closet, she kneeled down again and began sorting through the records. She found one they hadn't played in a long time and laid it on the turntable. Then, in an effort to waste as much time as possible, she slowly wound the arm and even changed the needle. But after the record had rasped and squealed for thirty seconds, Lizabeth couldn't bear any more of it and turned it off.

She went to the shelf and picked up a very old copy of *Robinson Crusoe*. Neither of them liked the story, but the pages of the book were yellowed, and its tiny print faded, so they added it to their collection for its "artistic value." Lizabeth returned with it to the fireplace. Then somehow, half reading, half staring into space, she managed to fight off the desire to run next door and find Loren.

What if she did go? What then, Lizabeth Elvira Bracken? Tell Loren that the V.I.G.'s and B.'s still meant more to her than he did? That L.E.B. had gone to Sharon's B.P. and meekly trailed along with them to throw eggs at his house? The only thing she hadn't done was actually throw an egg herself. Hurrah!

After two hours had passed, Lizabeth returned *Robinson Crusoe* carefully to its place on the shelf. She let the air out of the balloons and dropped them into the grocery sack. Then she removed the candles from the cupcakes, set the cakes back in their box, packed the box, the birthday gift, the cups, the napkins, and the thermos bottle of pink lemonade into the sack, picked it up, walked down the stairs and out the door, brushed the pebbles from the windowsill, and went home.

Chapter 14

THE NEXT AFTERNOON, Lizabeth returned to the house. She had no idea if Loren was going to be there. Perhaps he would. Perhaps he wouldn't. But she would wait there, and the next day she would go and wait there again if necessary. She knew she had to see him once more, not to excuse herself, because she felt there was no excuse, but only to say she was sorry. Whether it ever made any difference to him or not, she had to say it. And she would have to say it without cupcakes or candles, long skirts, or pink lemonade. She would say it just as she always was, Lizabeth, in her shorts and sneakers and summer-grubby knees.

She went right to the front door without putting pebbles on the windowsill. All that had ended now. She saw Nutsy sitting on the highest branch of his favorite oak tree deeply concerned with something he was eating. He didn't even look down, as if he had already forgotten about her.

Upstairs, in their room, Lizabeth went right to the bookshelf, picked up a battered copy of *The Adventures of Tom Sawyer,* a book she *did* like, and settled down with it by the fireplace. She tried not to let her eyes wander about the room. There was no point in making herself hurt all over again. At her side, she had laid the birthday gift for Loren. Just before she left the apartment, she had picked it up, set it down, picked it up, set it down, and then finally picked it up and brought it. Now she wished she had left it at home. There was no point in that either.

Once, a girl named Lizabeth might have been curled up on the floor of this house, lost in a book, with no thought at all of the passage of time. But today, though she was determined not to look at her watch, and thought that she was deeply engrossed in her story —she was turning the pages of the book, wasn't she?— her brain was ticking off every minute. And somewhere inside, she was listening to every tiny sound from outside the house. And then at last—she looked at her watch to find that, unbelievably, only twenty minutes had passed—she heard the sounds she was waiting for, the crunch of dried leaves on the veranda steps and the key turning in the lock.

And it was just then that Lizabeth knew she should have put pebbles on the windowsill after all. Without them, Loren couldn't know she was there. He wouldn't even have expected her there anyway. This was one of the days Sharon always came to swim at the Winston

156

Towers with Lizabeth. Loren knew that. But he didn't know that Sharon was going to be away for two days visiting her cousins. So if he was coming to the house, it must be because he was certain Lizabeth wasn't there. What would he say when he found her in the house—*his* house? How would he look? Lizabeth's heart seemed to be knocking the breath from her chest as she listened to his footsteps cross the floor beneath her, then climb the steps, his long legs taking them two and three at a time. She dropped her book and stood up to face him as he came through the door.

"Hey! What are you doing here? You're not supposed to be here today." Loren's face lighted up with his sudden, quick grin.

With that grin, the ten thousand tight little knots of misery and nothingness and fear inside Lizabeth vanished. This was not the stranger she had somehow been dreaming up for the past two days. This was Loren— Loren, grinning his old, familiar, *beautiful,* chip-toothed grin.

"I could come," was all Lizabeth could say.

"Boy, am I glad! I didn't even know you were here. I just came over to check up on everything. Hey! You know something? You looked scared when I came in. I didn't scare you, did I?"

"I didn't know if you'd like finding me here."

"Are you kidding? What gave you a crazy idea like that?"

Lizabeth hesitated. "You—you never came yesterday."

"Oh, my gosh!" Loren looked suddenly as if he'd

157

just been socked. "I tried to telephone you. I figured you'd be at that park thing you go to, but I tried anyway. Then I didn't know how else to reach you, so I put a note in the crack in the windowsill. It was crummy not to let you know until you got here, but I couldn't help it. Do you mean that you didn't get my note?"

Lizabeth shook her head. She had the overpowering urge to burst into tears and at the same time roll on the ground howling with laughter. The telephone call the morning before that couldn't be anyone important had been Loren!

"You mean you didn't even see it?" Loren was so surprised his voice was squeaking.

Lizabeth shook her head again.

"I don't understand that. Oh boy! Yes, I do!" Loren smacked his hand to his forehead. He strode determinedly to the window, stood looking out a moment, and then turned back to Lizabeth. "Nutsy! That overfed, thieving squirrel! I'll bet *he* took it. He'll help himself to anything that isn't nailed down. He's probably got it hidden in the drainpipe wondering what in heck to do with it. I think I'll go out there right now and—"

"Oh, don't! Please don't!" Lizabeth cried.

"Well, okay," Loren said. "But I'd really like to wring his little neck. You must have thought I was one wonderful person. What in heck *did* you think when I didn't show up?"

"I thought you didn't want to see me again after— after what happened the night before."

"Oh boy, that!" Loren's jaw tightened. "I guess you mean that mess on the front of our house. Prob-

158

ably one of Stickley's or Leggett's heroic ideas. Did everyone at the party come?"

"Yes."

"You too?"

"Yes."

"I suppose you had to come, didn't you?"

Lizabeth stared at a place just below Loren's chin, and shook her head slowly. "I didn't want to come, but I didn't have to. They didn't *make* me come. I could have said no."

"Ha!" Loren snorted. "Are you kidding? Look, you may think you got to choose about coming, but you didn't. With those characters, you don't get to choose anything. You do it their way, or else! So if you think I wouldn't want to see you again because of something like that, you're crazy. Hey! Would you wipe that scared look off your face? I'm not planning to eat you, honest."

He had finally succeeded in making Lizabeth smile.

"Why—why was it that you couldn't come?" she asked. Then she added quickly, "I mean, if you want to tell me." She had seen the smile on Loren's face fade suddenly.

"Yes, I want to tell you." He seemed to be having trouble swallowing. "Mimi had a stroke early yesterday morning. She's in the hospital now. It's just nutty. I don't even believe it."

"Oh, Loren!" It was all Lizabeth could say. She had never known that you could feel so numbed so suddenly.

"I couldn't reach my Aunt Mary in New York.

159

I got her answering service, but I had to wait by the telephone all day in case she called. I only left once to come over here to leave the note—for Nutsy, as it turned out."

"If I'd got it, I would have come over," Lizabeth said.

"To tell you the truth, I did wonder a little why you didn't. But anyway, Aunt Mary finally called, and then flew in last night. She's at the hospital with Mimi now." Loren drew in his breath sharply, and a shudder ran through him. "I don't know what's going to happen, Lizabeth. Oh boy! I'm scared!" Lizabeth saw tears well up in his eyes.

He turned quickly away from her, put his hands up on the mantel, and dropped his head so his face was half hidden by his arms. His voice cracked as he said again, "I'm scared!" With a quick, jerky motion, he rubbed his eyes against the cutoff sleeve of his sweat-shirt.

All her life, Lizabeth had always been the one to be comforted. She had never had to comfort anyone herself. She didn't know the proper words to say.

She raised her hand and hesitantly touched Loren's arm. Then, as she slowly dropped it, Loren's own hand came down from the mantel. Their hands touched and came together. Loren's hand closed around hers, and they stood that way, looking down into the empty fire-place, not saying anything.

Then Lizabeth felt Loren's hand tighten. "I'm glad you came."

"I am too," Lizabeth said.

"Boy-oh-boy!" Loren shuddered again. "Mimi's just got to get well. The doctor says it's not a bad stroke, and that Mimi's tough and a real fighter. But she's awful old, Lizabeth. You should have seen the way she looked yesterday morning."

"Mimi's not old!" Lizabeth said fiercely. "She doesn't even have gray hair!"

Loren turned to her. His cheeks were still wet, but he was grinning. "She dyes her hair! She doesn't know that I know it. It gets redder every week. What a faker!"

"Loren," Lizabeth said, "she'll get well. I know it!"

"Yeah! She will," Loren said.

They fell silent again.

"Hey!" Loren said suddenly. "What's that on the floor?"

"Your birthday present—in case you weren't mad at me."

"You really are a nut, you know that?" Loren grinned again. "Can I open it now?"

"You can't, but you *may*," said Lizabeth, primly imitating their teacher's English-class voice.

For a few moments, they went on standing there together, neither wanting to make the first move. Then finally, because it had to happen sometime, their fingers loosened and their hands fell apart, slowly.

In seconds, Loren had the paper and ribbons ripped off the package. "A new set of *The Lord of the Rings*!" His eyes were shining.

"It's only paperbacks," Lizabeth said apologetically.

"It's a lot nicer set than mine," Loren said. "And boy, can I use a replacement! My old set is really chewed up."

"I know. It's what you said before. That's why I got them."

"Thanks! I really mean it," Loren said.

"I'm sorry there aren't any refreshments," Lizabeth said. "I didn't bring *those* back today."

"I forgot that you were bringing stuff to eat yesterday. That's terrible—all that trouble and I didn't even show up. What a crumb!"

"It was only cupcakes and pink lemonade," Lizabeth said. "And I made the cupcakes from a mix. It wasn't hard."

"Could you bring them back again?" Loren asked.

Lizabeth laughed. "Not the same ones! The icing got all melted and icky. I'll make some more, though."

"That'd be great! But hey! Guess what?" Loren reached into his jeans pocket. "Here, take one. They aren't much, and they're kind of messy. I think they went through the laundry again!"

Loren might not think they were much, but to Lizabeth, a lemon Lifesaver that had come through the laundry in his pocket was at that moment the most wonderful-tasting thing she had ever had in her whole life!

Chapter 15

TWO DAYS LATER, Lizabeth lied to Sharon. It was one big blanket lie to save herself telling a dozen small ones to keep her days free so she could go to the secret house. Until she was certain that Mimi was going to be well again, Lizabeth intended to be with Loren every chance she could. So she informed Sharon that she was going to baby-sit for Mrs. Dawes all day every day for two weeks.

The lie didn't bother her nearly so much as it might have, because deep inside, she couldn't help feeling that Sharon was somehow to blame for what happened at her party, or at least might have tried to stop it. It didn't matter that she'd never told Sharon any of this.

The days that followed right after Mimi became ill were quiet ones at the house. They were filled with reading by the fireplace, or sitting and talking on the veranda steps, or making visits to the stream, where they sat on their heels, silently watching the patterns made by strange, long-legged insects dancing across the surface of the water.

Then one afternoon Loren came bursting up the stairs shouting, "Hey! Guess what? Mimi asked for her hair kit today! I think she's afraid someone will discover she's getting a couple of gray hairs. What a phony baloney!" Loren was grinning so hard that Lizabeth thought his face would split. That afternoon, for the first time in days, they played records on the old Gramophone, happily covering their ears and smiling at one another when the screeching and wailing became too much for them.

That was when Lizabeth could stop thinking about Mimi long enough to start thinking a lot, and feeling guilty, about Sharon and the lie. She had gone to dinner one night at the Eberhards', and had talked to Sharon several times at night on the telephone, but there were no swimming dates. Before then, Sharon had been regularly coming over on the three days a week when she didn't baby-sit or have baton-twirling lessons or have to go visit one of her ten million cousins. Sometimes Lizabeth got tired of opening the front door to Sharon in her pink bikini and lemon-yellow beach towel. She wondered once, fleetingly, if their whole friendship weren't founded on the Winston Towers swimming pool. But that still didn't make her feel any more comfortable about the lie. She hadn't even told Loren about it, because she wasn't certain he'd approve.

164

So she just told him Sharon was going to be busy for a couple of weeks, and let it go at that. But the lie really was beginning to bother her. The two-week baby-sitting date supposedly wasn't up yet, when Lizabeth decided that she would call Sharon and tell her that they could have their swimming afternoons together again.

She would call her that evening, she told herself as she unlocked the door to the house. Loren would groan when she told him that Sharon was back in the picture again, but he'd understand. After all, he was the one who kept telling her, "Sharon first. Loren second." The way it was with the birthday parties.

The house seemed so quiet that day, Lizabeth thought, quieter than usual, as if it were holding its breath. But she knew that Loren was upstairs. Three pebbles lay on the windowsill. Why did they always use three? she wondered. They had never discussed numbers, for goodness sake. It was something she would have to ask Loren about.

Reading! The house was so quiet because Loren was reading, with his nose so deep in a book he probably didn't even hear her. Lizabeth smiled. She wondered if it would be unfair to tiptoe into the room.

She found Loren sitting in front of the fireplace, his arms on his knees, his shoulders hunched over. There was no book in front of him. He was just sucking absently on a stalk of sour grass. When he looked up at Lizabeth, it wasn't with his usual grin, the one that came so suddenly it was almost always a surprise to her, like a lovely present she wasn't expecting. Seeing him now brought a funny stab inside her.

"Is Mimi all right?" It was the first thought that jumped into her head. "Has something happened?"

"Mimi's okay, honest," Loren said. He paused a moment. "But we're leaving, Lizabeth."

"Leaving?" Lizabeth repeated it dimly, as if it were some foreign word that she needed someone to translate for her. "Do you mean, going away?"

"Yes," Loren said. "To stay."

To stay! That meant *never to come back,* didn't it? As the words became coldly clearer, Lizabeth's legs seemed to crumple beneath her. She sank to her knees beside Loren. To stay! But that sounded so *final.*

"Forever? Will you go away forever?" she said in a whisper.

Loren shrugged. "Aunt Mary seems to think so. That's where we're going, to New York to live with my aunt and uncle. Their apartment is big enough for all of us, I guess."

"I don't understand. I thought Mimi was getting well. You said she was all right."

"She is," Loren said. "But I guess a stroke, even a little one, isn't something you get over like a cold, especially when you're as old as Mimi. She calls herself a spring chicken, but she isn't. She can't just come back and start looking after a house. The doctor says she's going to need someone to look after *her,* maybe for a long time." He hesitated a moment. "Hey! You know something funny? When I lost my mom and dad, I was supposed to go live with Aunt Mary and Uncle Carl, but Mimi won out. It wasn't much of a struggle. They've never liked kids too much. Looks like they're getting me after all!" He smiled hopefully at Lizabeth as if he expected a smile in return. It was a rueful, wistful smile, but it was a smile nonetheless.

How could he find anything funny about all of this? she wondered. Did he expect her to smile back when everything inside her was smashed into sharp, splintered bits like a crushed Christmas-tree ball?

From the beginning, her friendship with Loren had gone up and down, up and down, as if it were on a wild roller-coaster ride. But what was the use if in the end it was going to come crashing down and stay there? Why hadn't Loren just let her leave the very first time they met in the house? She would have got over the loss of the house easily enough in time. What had been the point of all of it?

"Why are you looking like that?" Loren said suddenly. "Do you think I *want* to go?"

For some strange reason that she would never understand, that was all Lizabeth needed to make her know exactly what the point of all of it had been. She managed a timid, hesitant smile. "No, I know you don't."

They were still smiling at one another when Loren said, "I guess I've known for some time that this might happen. Aunt Mary has been trying to drum it into me. But I didn't want to ruin all this. Anyway, I kept hoping something would change. Now I know it isn't going to." He stopped talking and shrugged. "Mimi says we're coming back, Lizabeth."

"Do you think you will?"

"Who knows? But I know *I'm* coming back. Mr.

Sumner has invited me to come stay with him and his wife any time I want to. He says"—Loren dropped his chin and lowered his voice as if he were about to make an important speech—"I will want to return to visit my many friends!" Loren looked hugely amused over this. "That's you, I guess. I mean, if you're interested, many friends!"

"I'm interested!" said Lizabeth.

"The only thing is," Loren went on, "Mr. Sumner says the house has to be boarded up again—I mean, really boarded up, and locked up so no one can come in. I'm really sorry, Lizabeth."

"It's all right," Lizabeth said, and she meant it. She had learned that the house wasn't anything without Loren in it. It hardly seemed possible that once, long ago, she had actually wanted it all to herself. Now there was something far more important than learning what was to happen to the house.

"How long—how long before you leave?"

"Not long. Less than a week, maybe," Loren said.

Less than a week, maybe.

With that thought pounding dully in her head, Lizabeth hardly remembered her walk home from the house or through the Winston Towers lobby, or her ride up in the padded vinyl elevator. And she never did remember that she was going to call Sharon. Even if she had, it wouldn't have made any difference.

Lizabeth was lying on her bed staring blankly at the ceiling, when she heard the ringing in the kitchen. It was probably her mother, she thought, calling as she often did to say she'd be a little late coming home. Would Lizabeth be a sweetie and turn on the oven or set the table or see if they needed any milk? With a weary little sigh, Lizabeth rose and went to answer the telephone.

"Hello."

"Hello, this is Sharon," said a voice that sounded curiously not like Sharon's.

"Oh, hi, Sharon," said Lizabeth. She knew that she was stuck now with carrying on a bright, cheerful conversation for half an hour or more. Unless, of course, she could come up with some good reason to get out of it. "I—I guess I can't talk too long," she said. "I'm expecting a call from Mother."

"That's all right," said Sharon. She still sounded strange, as if she were weighing and measuring every word. "I only wanted to know"—pause—"if you had a good time this afternoon."

Lizabeth felt her throat tighten. "Good time?"

"I meant baby-sitting," said Sharon.

"Oh, that!" Lizabeth gave a little laugh. "I guess it was all right. You don't exactly have a wonderful, exciting time baby-sitting."

"Oh," said Sharon. There was a longer pause. "Well then, did you have a—a better time baby-sitting *yesterday?*"

"I don't know," Lizabeth said. "I never thought about it. That's a funny question, Sharon."

This time there was such a long pause that Lizabeth wondered if Sharon had left the telephone. "I don't think it's so funny," Sharon's strained voice said

169

at last. "I happen to know you weren't baby-sitting this afternoon, Lizabeth."

⌐Lizabeth's heart smacked against her chest. "Well —well then, if I wasn't baby-sitting, where was I?"

"I don't know," said Sharon. "I just know you weren't baby-sitting."

"Where did you find that out?"

"From Mrs. Dawes—when I called."

There was a silence. "Why did you call Mrs. Dawes?" Lizabeth asked stiffly.

"I didn't call Mrs. Dawes. I called her number to talk to you." Sharon waited a moment for this to settle. "I know you don't think it's right to have phone calls when you're baby-sitting, but my cousin Laura is going to be here for just two hours tonight on her way to visit a friend. I've—I've told her a lot about you, so I wanted her to meet you. When I called, I didn't know I was going to get Mrs. Dawes. She told me that you weren't there, and that you only baby-sit two mornings a week, like always. You never come in the afternoons at all!" Sharon took a deep breath. "Why did you make up that story, Lizabeth?"

Why did Lizabeth make up that story? Because of *Sharon,* that's why, Sharon and all her precious V.I.G.'s and B.'s. It was Sharon who had forced her into this trap, and now sat there accusing her of making up stories and telling lies!

"Well, why did you call me there, Sharon?" She was trying to keep her voice from shaking. "You shouldn't have called me there."

"I told you why I did," Sharon said. "Anyway,"

170

she flung out, "you should have told me where you were."

"Why should I?" Lizabeth hurled back. "I don't have to tell you everywhere I go and everything I do."

"Best friends do, Lizabeth. They tell each other everything!"

Then, in an absolutely calm, even voice, Lizabeth replied, "Who ever said we were best friends, Sharon?"

There was utter silence on the other end of the telephone. Lizabeth waited a few moments. Her hand grew icy and wet on the receiver. Then she set it down with a firm click. She ran back to her room and hurled herself on her bed. And the tears she hadn't been able to cry since she'd come home that afternoon finally poured down her cheeks.

Chapter 16

ONLY THE SOUND of a stray bee buzzing lonesomely over the wild honeysuckle broke the silence of the hot summer afternoon when Lizabeth arrived at the house for the last time. Pebbles were already lying on the windowsill—for the last time, Lizabeth told herself. She unlocked the door with her still-shiny key, moved slowly past the stiff, worn old rocking chairs, and listened to the funny stick-stick sound her sneakers made as she walked up the stairs, all for the last time. And she remembered, with a heart-stopping feeling, as she walked through the door and found Loren standing by the fireplace grinning at her, that *that* was for the last time too.

But she made herself smile, because she was coming to a farewell party Loren had insisted on giving for *her*. "The last social event of the season!" he said. "Heck, I'm privileged to give it." Lizabeth felt that she owed it to him to smile.

He had already laid out on the floor place mats, paper cups and plates, and two larger plates, one piled with gingerbread boys and the other with sandwiches. Beside one place setting, on the side where Lizabeth usually sat, was an envelope and a package, not too neatly wrapped in white tissue paper and a large red bow.

"Before you get too excited about it," Loren said, "those gingerbread boys came from the local bakery. I did, however"—he puffed on his fingernails and polished them on his shirt—"make the sandwiches. By hand, that is! Would you like to ask me what kind they are?"

"What kind are they?" Lizabeth asked dutifully.

"Watercress! And you'd better like them. Would you like to know how many grocery stores don't have watercress? Six—at least! Watercress!" Loren grimaced.

"I'll love them, I promise," Lizabeth said. "My very first watercress sandwiches!"

"The gingerbread boys were Mimi's idea," Loren said. "She remembered when you were telling her about the gingerbread on your summer house. She said since we never provided any with this house, I should buy you some, which I did."

"I wish I could have seen Mimi again before you leave."

"She wishes it too, but Aunt Mary is guarding her like a hawk. She sent you a note, though."

"Should I read it now?" Lizabeth asked.

"You're supposed to," Loren said. "But, hey! Why

173

don't you open the package first. *That's* from me!" He handed her the awkwardly wrapped package with the big red bow.

Lizabeth untied the bow and peeled off the paper with great deliberation as Loren watched her impatiently. "Oh, Loren! It's Nutsy!"

"A pretty good model of him, I guess," Loren said.

"He's much better than a pretty good model," Lizabeth said indignantly. "He's exactly like him. Look at that bushy tail and the black eyes. Loren, he's beautiful!" She put the plush squirrel up to her cheeks, hugging him. "I love him!"

"Hey! Why don't you open the note now," Loren said. He was blushing.

Lizabeth set the squirrel down reluctantly and picked up the note. Then she opened it and read:

My dear Lizabeth,

I hope you will excuse this very bad writing. My hand is not quite steady as yet. However, I do want to tell you, dear child, how much your friendship has meant to Loren, and to me too. You are one very good reason why we shall try hard to return one day. In the meantime, Loren is already making very definite plans to come back for a visit, courtesy of my kind lawyer, Mr. Sumner.

I am sorry that this same Mr. Sumner does not think it proper, or safe, for you to come visiting "your house" while I am not living next to it, but I must confess that I see the wisdom in his decision.

174

I see no reason why you and a friend might not come to visit the front steps sometime, though, or the rest of the grounds around the house, and have so informed Mr. Sumner. It would give me great pleasure to know that you were doing so.

You have often referred to "your house" as a magic house. It is indeed, for having brought you to us!

> *Affectionately,*
> *Mimi*

—When Lizabeth had finished reading the note, she quickly picked up the squirrel and made a great pretense of studying him carefully.

"Mimi means that, about bringing someone to visit the house someday," Loren said, filling the silence for her. "Maybe—maybe when I'm gone, you could bring Sharon."

"Sharon wouldn't want to come," Lizabeth said, and then because it had sounded like such a rude thing to say, added in her confusion something she had not told Loren. "I mean, we've had a fight."

Loren looked at her sharply. "Not about me, I hope! It wasn't about me, was it?"

"No, it was—it was about something else."

"What something else?" Loren persisted. "Lizabeth, it must have had something to do with me. If it hadn't, you would have told me about it. Look, I want you to tell me!"

So Lizabeth finally did, starting with the lie.

175

When she'd finished, Loren shook his head and said under his breath, "Boy-oh-boy! You shouldn't have done that, not for me, Lizabeth."

"Why not?" Lizabeth said. "I haven't lost a very good friend, so what difference does it make?"

"I'll tell you what difference it makes!" Loren sounded as if he were grinding the words through his teeth. "Look, I've never told you how I got to be Creepy Douglas. Haven't you ever wondered about that?"

Lizabeth flung her head back. "I don't care how you got to be *anything!* I don't want to hear about it."

"Well, I think you ought to," Loren said evenly. "So I'm going to tell you, and you're going to listen. You know, I wasn't just all of a sudden Creepy Douglas when I first came to Anderson Bays in fourth grade. Most of the kids liked me pretty well at first. But then Mrs. Mason, our teacher, kept making a big fuss over me. She was really nice, and I know she was just feeling sorry for me because of what happened to Mom and Dad, and because I was new and all that. But it sure didn't go over with the class when she kept choosing me to do everything—you know, take notes to the office and all that. On top of it all, I got good grades, which didn't help any.

"But the big blow came when they had a class election, and a guy nominated me for president. Boy-oh-boy, was that stupid! Anyway, the big class leader then was a boy called Peter Harkney. He'd never paid much attention to me, but I guess he'd liked me okay up until then. Well, after that, he started *not* liking me. And suddenly I started having pretty few friends, and

176

then no friends at all. I never was sure what was happening until one day Peter and two other guys started pushing me around in school, and I could see whose idea it all was. Anyway, that was when they found out something else about me—I don't fight back. After that, my life was worth about nothing at school. They jumped me every chance they had. Once they got me down and just about blew my eardrums out with a trumpet. It was really great!" Loren paused, biting his lip, as if he were remembering how it felt.

"Did Mimi know about it?" Lizabeth asked.

"Not at first. Then one day I came home all banged up. Naturally she was going to rush right down and see the principal, but I talked her out of it. In the end, she agreed it was better not to, and marched me into town to take some judo lessons instead." Loren shook his head, grinning. "No luck. I was okay as long as I was working with the instructor, not bad in fact. But as soon as I really had to throw someone, I froze. I just stood there and let those little guys that came up to my belly button sock me to the ground. So much for judo! After that, I ended up doing what any red-blooded, all-American chicken would do when those guys at school came after me—I ran!"

"Is that why"—Lizabeth hesitated—"why you didn't do anything that time behind stage when Dennis put paint on you? I wanted you to take the brush and paint his *face* with it!"

"Do you think I didn't want to? Or pull the curtain across that stupid act of theirs? But I value my life, Lizabeth."

Loren's voice was grim, and it gave Lizabeth a sudden, odd feeling in the pit of her stomach to see his knuckles whiten in a helpless, angry fist, just as they had that terrible night backstage.

"I don't understand," she said. "You don't mind doing dangerous things like climbing out on the veranda roof. Why couldn't you fight those boys?"

"Because I'm not afraid of stuff like climbing on roofs or getting an arm or leg busted. I'm just afraid of tackling people—or maybe I don't want to. I don't know. Anyway, even if I did want to fight, those guys always stick together. If you fight one, you have to fight two or three. Peter Harkney never came at me alone. He always had one or two other guys with him. Anyway, that's how it all got started, back in the fourth grade, and the whole idea got inherited into the fifth grade, and then into the sixth. Peter Harkney isn't even here anymore, but would you like to guess who his two friends were?"

"Tom Leggett and Dennis Stickley?"

"Right! But the point is that just one guy started it all, Lizabeth—just one guy! I don't want that to happen to you."

"They wouldn't beat up on me," Lizabeth said. "I mean, they wouldn't punch me or sock me or anything like that."

"No, they wouldn't do that to a girl, but there are lots of other ways they can beat up on you that don't show on the outside. Look, Lizabeth, I'm going to a new school. It's going to be different for me. But you're staying right here with these guys. I'm going to feel terrific

178

leaving and knowing that you killed yourself with them because of me. You've got to get back together with Sharon. You've just *got* to!"

Loren was right. Lizabeth knew that if Sharon would have her, she had to go back. Which meant going back to a friendship of hiding things, of saying what she needed to, and acting the way she was expected to, of going all the way back to being L.E.B.

"Hey! Why don't you go see her right now?"

"Now?"

"Sure, now! Look, you want me to leave a happy guy, don't you?"

"But I can't!" Lizabeth cried. "I don't want to! This is our last afternoon, and I don't want to spend it with someone else."

"I didn't mean you had to spend the whole afternoon there, nut! It would only take you five minutes to go to Sharon's house. You wouldn't be gone more than half an hour or so. I'll wait for you here, I promise. All this stuff can wait until you get back. On my honor, I won't touch the watercress sandwiches. Please go, Lizabeth. Please!"

Loren jumped up, then took Lizabeth's hand and pulled her up beside him.

"She might not be home," Lizabeth said hopefully.

"So come back. Then try later and write me about it."

"I don't know what to say to her."

"Just tell her you're sorry for what happened and you want to be friends again. Very simple."

"Well, what—what if she asks me what I was

doing when I wasn't baby-sitting? What then?" Lizabeth asked.

The question stumped Loren for a moment. He apparently hadn't thought about that possibility. "Tell her about the house, Lizabeth. Just don't tell her about me. She doesn't have to know about me—ever."

Loren took Lizabeth by the shoulders and turned her toward the door. "Now move! I'll be waiting for you. And remember, just don't tell her about me. Okay?"

"Okay," Lizabeth said dimly.

But it was only the thought of Loren standing there and smiling his encouragement in the empty room that made her able to walk down the stairs and out of the house.

Chapter 17

IT WAS MRS. EBERHARD who answered the doorbell when Lizabeth rang. She was in faded blue baggy slacks, and her hands were coated with black grease, as if she'd been busy repairing something. It didn't seem to bother her a bit that she'd been called from whatever she was doing just for Lizabeth.

"Hi, honey, come on in! Sharon's in her room. You go right on upstairs."

"Thank you," said Lizabeth. She returned what she hoped was a perfectly ordinary happy smile, and went up the stairs. At the top, she had to draw in a deep breath as if she had just climbed a very steep hill.

The door to Sharon's room was closed, so Lizabeth knocked.

"Who is it?"

"It's me, Lizabeth. May I come in?"

There was a silence. "Yes."

Lizabeth took another deep breath, and opened the door.

Sharon was sitting on the edge of her bed in front of a card table with a tablet of drawing paper on it. Beside the tablet was a box of pastel crayons and a picture turned face down. Lizabeth recognized the frame as the one that was around the picture of the two of them that her mother had sketched. It appeared, from what Lizabeth could see on the tablet, that Sharon had been trying to copy the picture.

Sharon twisted a crayon between her fingers. "Hi!"

"Hi!" said Lizabeth. She stepped into the room.

Then nobody said anything.

"That's good. I didn't know you could draw like that." Lizabeth's voice came out strange and loud in Sharon's small room.

Sharon didn't seem to notice it. "I've never tried before. I—I think it's terrible."

"No, it isn't. It's good! I'd like—I'd like my mother to see it," Lizabeth said, and then without stopping, as if she were racing through a rehearsed speech, added, "I'm sorry I said what I did, Sharon. If—if you'd like it, I'd like to be friends again."

Sharon laid her crayon down carefully beside her drawing tablet. "I'd like it. It was all my fault. I shouldn't have called you up and asked questions. It wasn't any of my business. You don't have to tell me everything, Lizabeth, if you don't want to."

Lizabeth sat down on the little bench in front of Sharon's dresser and folded her hands in her lap. "I

182

want to tell you about where I was when you called Mrs. Dawes."

"I said you didn't have to!" Sharon blurted out.

"I want to," said Lizabeth, and went right on. "I discovered an old house where nobody lives anymore. I found that I could get into it, and—and that's where I've been going all along!"

"A house?" Sharon said. "I don't understand. Why didn't you want to tell me about an old house?"

"It starts from a long time ago," Lizabeth said. "Do you remember that day I was late to school and told you I'd been to the eye doctor and needed glasses?"

"Yes," Sharon said.

"I told you later I didn't need them after all—that the doctor said I could wait before I got them. Do you remember?"

Sharon nodded.

Lizabeth found she had to swallow before she could go on. "Well, it was all a lie! I never went to the doctor at all. I don't even know why I said it. I'd been crying that morning, and I didn't want you to know."

"What's wrong with crying?" Sharon asked. "Everybody cries sometimes."

"But *I* was crying because I'd just been told we weren't going to the summer house. When I first told you about the summer house, you laughed about it as if it were so funny. I didn't want you to laugh at me again!"

Sharon stared down at the picture she'd begun on the tablet. Then all at once she flung back her head. "Yes, I did laugh then! And I did think it was funny!

183

Wouldn't you if you *lived* in an old house? This is a dumpy, messy old house, and I live in it all the time, Lizabeth!" Suddenly, Sharon's eyes were filled with tears. "And in the summer, do you know what *we* do? Mama—I mean, *Mother* bakes pies and cakes and cookies and fills big pots with soup and stew. Then she and Daddy and the twins and Lynda and I all pile into the station wagon and go visit my Aunt May and Uncle Frank and our five cousins. They live in an old dumpy house just like this one. And *that's* why I thought what you said was so funny!"

"But I like your house!" Lizabeth cried. "I like to come here. It's—it's comfortable!"

"You don't live here!" Sharon flung back. "It's different to just visit someplace than to live in it. You live in a nice, neat place where everything is pretty and new and shiny. You have *glass* tables in the living room! Your room looks like—like fresh snow's just fallen on it with everything clean and white." And then Sharon said wistfully, "There's just you and your mother and father. And your mother is pretty and paints pictures and works at an art gallery, and your father says funny things and—and wears turtleneck shirts and blazers. I love my family, but they're not like yours, Lizabeth."

Lizabeth suddenly found something very interesting to do with her fingernails. "You've never said anything about it, Sharon."

"You don't say things like how you feel about your mother looking like a big, crumpled grocery sack, or your father going around showing his cutoff finger to everyone. There—there are lots of things you don't say."

Lizabeth continued with her fingernail work. "Maybe we ought to say them. I mean, sometimes."

"Maybe we ought to," Sharon said.

There was a long silence as they both considered the meaning of this. Then Lizabeth looked at her watch.

"I don't want to go now, but I guess I have to. There's—there's someone waiting for me at the house."

"Is it—" Sharon ran a finger down the edge of her drawing tablet. "Is it a new friend?" Then she reddened and said quickly, "I mean, you don't have to tell me if you don't want to!"

"Yes, it's a new friend. It's—*he's* a boy."

"Oh!" Sharon's eyebrows flew up, but it seemed to take her a moment to find the courage to say, "Do I know him?"

"You know who he is," Lizabeth said, "but—but you don't really know him."

A sudden picture of Loren flashed into her mind—Loren standing in the room alone giving her an encouraging smile and sending her off to make up with someone who considered him Creepy Douglas, Loren with his intent blue eyes and infectious chip-toothed grin, who smelled sweetly of Ivory soap, and was kind and nice and fun and funny—Loren, who had made the secret house the magic house! No, Sharon didn't really know him, so it wasn't a lie to say so.

But she was looking at Lizabeth curiously, so before she had a chance to ask another question, Lizabeth

186

raced on. "Anyway, he's going away tomorrow, so I guess it really doesn't matter. The house turned out to be his, or at least his family's, and we've been fixing it up together. When he leaves, I won't be able to go into it anymore. I'll only be able to visit the outside."

"Would you take me sometime? I mean, you don't have to—" Sharon stopped in confusion.

"I'd love to take you, if you'd like to come," Lizabeth said, smiling. "We could go tomorrow, if you'd like. I'll call you tonight, okay?"

"Okay," Sharon said.

Lizabeth started for the door, but even before she got there, she knew the conversation hadn't really been ended. There were still words that had to be said—perhaps not today, or even tomorrow, but sometime.

She had discovered that Sharon was as afraid of losing her friendship as she'd been of losing Sharon's, that Sharon was afraid of a lot of things, just as she was. And just as *all* the V.I.G.'s and B.'s probably were, all afraid of losing each other, of losing their place in the magic circle.

But knowing all this wouldn't make it any easier to say the words. Anyway, the V.I.G.'s and B.'s really had nothing to do with it anymore. This had to do with three people—Loren, Lizabeth, and Sharon.

There *was* a friendship she could have with Sharon, Lizabeth knew now, even if it wasn't one that had to do with dolls or exchanging sunflower seeds and carrot sticks or swinging across bars on the playground. There were other kinds of friendships that came with being twelve. And for the sake of that friendship, as

187

well as to prove once and forever to Loren what *his* friendship meant to her, Lizabeth had to say those words. The only question was, when would she have the courage to say them?

At the doorway, Lizabeth stopped once more to smile at Sharon. Then suddenly, before she could stop herself, she heard her voice saying over the pounding of her heart, "If you're not too busy, would you like to go with me to the house now, Sharon?"

And it seemed as if from the very beginning she had known it would happen this way.

OTHER BOOKS BY BARBARA BROOKS WALLACE

Andrew the Big Deal
Can Do, Missy Charlie
Claudia
Victoria

About the Author

WHEN BARBARA BROOKS WALLACE STARTED WRITING for children, it seemed to her that all children's authors had known they wanted to write at a very early age and had done so, or they had been children's librarians or teachers, or had had piles of children. Mrs. Wallace felt she had none of the proper credentials. She had written only one poem as a child and wasn't too impressed with it, and she hadn't *been* any of the right things, and she had only one son. It was all very discouraging.

But, happily for herself and for thousands of her young readers, she persisted in her writing, creating several children's books that have been very well received by critics and children alike. *The Secret Summer of L.E.B.* is her fifth book published by Follett.

Mrs. Wallace was born and raised in China, where her American-born father was a businessman and her Russian-born mother was a nurse. She attended schools in China and had crossed the Pacific nine times before coming to live in the United States. One of these crossings followed a frightening experience when she and her sister, under the care of a lady missionary doctor, were cut off from her parents in Shanghai by the start of Japanese activity in World War II. The girls had to be evacuated later from China on an American destroyer.

Mrs. Wallace graduated from the University of California at Los Angeles and worked for a Los Angeles advertising agency and radio station for a time. She now lives with her husband, a former air force officer, and their teenaged son, Jimmy, in Alexandria, Virginia.